D1548837

A RISKY INTERLUDE

"I've never met a young lady who could quote Shakespeare, or who even wished to read him. You're different," Valin said.

The sound of his voice zinged from her ears to her spine! She had to get away from him and compose herself. Drat. What was wrong with her that she couldn't play a part she'd managed easily in the past?

"You have mysteries about you, Miss Emily de Winter, and I'm going to solve them."

"What fancies, my lord." Emmie lifted her skirts and walked up the stairs that led to the front door of Agincourt Hall.

North mounted the stairs two at a time and planted himself in front of her. "You're unnerved. I can see a tiny vein throbbing at your temple, and you're breathing as hard as if you'd ridden in the Derby." He narrowed his eyes as he regarded her. "I'm onto something, by Jove. And it's important, by the look of you. Who would have thought?" She tried to go around him, but he stepped in her way, bent over her, and smiled lazily.

"What are you hiding, Miss Emily de Winter?"

The Treasure

Suzanne Robinson

BANTAM BOOKS
New York Toronto London Sydney Auckland

THE TREASURE

A Bantam Book / April 1999

All rights reserved.
Copyright © 1999 by Suzanne Robinson.
Cover art copyright © 1999 by Alan Ayers.
Cover insert art copyright © 1999 by Lina Levy.

ISBN 0-553-57958-4

Bantam Books are published by Bantam Books, a division of
Random House, Inc. Its trademark, consisting of the words "Bantam
Books" and the portrayal of a rooster, is Registered in U.S. Patent
and Trademark Office and in other countries. Marca Registrada.
Bantam Books, 1540 Broadway, New York, New York 10036.

PRINTED IN THE UNITED STATES OF AMERICA

OPM   10 9 8 7 6 5 4 3 2 1

There are some people who face life with cour-age, defy hardship, and provide loving support to all around them. My aunt, Georgia May Womack, has done this for me and my family. This book is dedicated to her with love and gratitude.

1

London, 1860

No one in Society thought Valin North had any right to be as disgruntled and miserable as he appeared. When he wasn't glowering at someone, people agreed to call him handsome. Certainly he was rich, titled, and endowed with polished manners—when he bothered to employ them—and intelligence, and a family untouched by scandal.

Thus on this fine April evening those invited by his aunt to a musical party at North's town house found it unpardonable that their host wore a perpetually volcanic expression on his face. For his part, Valin Edward St. John North, Marquess of Westfield, wouldn't have cared had he noticed that the various Society biddies clustered about the drawing room disapproved. He was in agony.

Aunt Ottoline had invited yet another flock of eligible young ladies for him to meet, and Lady Millicent Amberley had cornered him. Valin winced as her voice attacked his defenseless ears. Lady Millicent was a racing champion of talkers; she rattled, babbled, and blathered without seeming to take a breath. Valin fixed his gaze on her flapping lips and in a dazed manner wondered that she could find so much to say about nothing.

"And of course for summer I must have gowns of dimity, lawn, and chambray. For winter I prefer cashmere, merino, brocade, and velvet."

Valin cursed his aunt. Lady Millicent might have a fortune and be the daughter of a duke, but no amount of aristocratic resources made up for her babbling. When she began to describe her preferences in fabrics for evening wear, his brows met in the center of his forehead. He fixed her with his most frightening scowl, but Lady Millicent was entranced with the sound of her own words. *FinenettedtullegauzetransparenttarlatanLyonssilk.* The words ran together like the waters of a flood, causing Valin's head to hurt.

Then, just as he was about to bark at his tormentor, he felt a strange prickling along his spine, as though battalions of ants were beating a retreat down it. He looked up, over the heads of his guests, past footmen serving wine and finger sandwiches. Finally his gaze fastened on an old lady shrouded in mourning dress. She had white hair arranged in old-fashioned corkscrew curls and was wearing tinted spectacles.

The peculiar creature was staring at him. Society ladies didn't stare, at least, not openly. When their eyes met, she didn't look away, but regarded him with composure through those smoky glass lenses. He glared back, expecting her to turn red and avert her gaze. Instead she squinted at him and smirked as if she knew how irritated he was and why.

Valin swore to himself as he felt heat rising from his neck to his cheeks. No one smirked at him! Least of all pink-cheeked little old ladies shaped like plums. He would not be smirked at, by heaven. Battle-hardened soldiers in the Crimea had melted into their boots under his glare. His menacing stare would have been at home stalking gazelles on the plains of Africa. How dare she smirk at him as if he were a disgruntled street urchin?

Renewing his efforts, Valin furrowed his brow, narrowed his eyes, and pulled himself up to his full height so that he could look down on the offending lady from the greatest altitude possible. He summoned a glower that belonged to a raging god on Olympus and impaled the old woman with it.

To his astonishment, the lady's veined nose wrinkled, and she did something he could hardly believe. She sniggered at him!

Valin started toward the old woman, but Lady Millicent's voice stopped him.

"I know you'll appreciate the lace on my gown, my lord. It's Honiton."

His eyes widening, Valin growled and spun on his heel, leaving Millicent to gape at wide shoulders covered in an immaculate evening coat. He took refuge in a group of older men clustered near the fireplace. There a place of honor had been reserved for Tuppy Swanwick, a family friend and ancient veteran of the Napoleanic wars. Valin tried to master his foul humor while listening yet again to Tuppy's story of how he'd lost his leg at Waterloo. He could feel the tension draining from his body as he half attended to Tuppy's quavering voice, and he'd almost forgotten about the inane Lady Millicent when that unusual old lady walked by in the company of other black-clad dowagers. As she passed she shot a look of amusement at him.

"I see what you mean, Mrs. Whichelo. Permanently ill-tempered indeed."

Valin's mouth dropped open, but before he could collect himself, the ladies passed out of the room and into the salon. Valin excused himself and followed them, but everyone was gathering to hear the pianist Aunt Ottoline had asked to perform this evening, and he lost sight of the woman in the crowd. Rows of gilded chairs filled the long chamber, and he was commandeered by his brother Acton to join the family in the front row.

He sat down and twisted his neck to peer at the guests filing in, but the old lady was nowhere to be seen. He glimpsed a black gown beaded with jet disappearing behind a fern near the door, but Aunt Ottoline slapped him on the arm with her fan and hissed at him.

"Saints and Providence give me patience!"

"What?"

"You were rude to Lady Millicent after all the trouble I took to get her here."

Valin's scowl returned. "She's a blatherer."

"A what?"

"A blatherer. She drones on and on, endlessly, about nothing. I can't marry her. I'd shoot her on the honeymoon."

"Oh, Valin!"

Ottoline's voice rose to a whispering screech that reminded Valin of an angry parrot: hoarse and ear-splittingly loud. He watched her master her irritation with difficulty.

"And what about the Honorable Miss Gorst?"

"Too religious. She should have been a nun."

Ottoline pursed her lips. "You can't say that about Lady Gladys."

"Lady Gladys is stupid."

"Va—lin," Ottoline growled.

"It's not my fault. The woman thinks Scutari is an Italian dessert and that Istanbul is a kind of cow."

Aunt Ottoline closed her eyes briefly before soldiering on. "Then what about Miss Hayhoe?"

"Miss Hayhoe possesses tact and intelligence."

His aunt began to smile.

"Unfortunately she laughs like a zebra."

"Oh, Valin!"

"Never mind that," Valin said before his aunt could embark on a scolding. "Who is that curious old dowager in the tinted spectacles?"

"Really, Valin, I can't keep introducing you to young ladies and have you chew them up and spit them out. Soon no one will allow you to meet his daughter despite your rank and fortune."

"Aunt, who is the lady in the tinted spectacles?"

"Spectacles? Oh, a friend of Lady Buxton's down from the North Country. The Honorable Miss Agnes Cowper, I think her name was. She rarely comes to town. Prefers the wilds of Northumberland."

"Don't invite her here again."

Ottoline slapped him with her fan again. "Nonsense. I can't invite Lady Buxton and not include her guest. It isn't done. Really, Valin, your manners are growing more and more barbaric. It's the war. I told you not to go. You didn't have to serve.

I'll admit you were gloomy and ill-tempered before you went, but when you came back you'd turned into a snarling beast."

Valin ceased listening to his aunt's complaints. They were well rehearsed, and he wasn't about to tell her the truth. He'd hidden it, buried it deep in his soul where it festered and corrupted his life, kept it silent since that day of horror when he was seventeen. The rest of the family didn't need to know what had really happened, and he deserved to carry the burden of his guilt alone.

Dragging his thoughts back to the present, Valin found that he was still furious at that bespectacled old lady for routing him. The next time he saw her, he'd teach her not to smirk at him. He'd reduce her to a quivering blancmange with his most terrifying grimace. The triumph would recompense him for the torture of looking for a suitable wife—a wife he didn't want or merit.

❧

The Honorable Agnes Cowper hobbled from behind the giant fern as the pianist began to play. With little mincing steps she left the salon and mounted the curved staircase. Several young ladies hurried past her on their way to the concert, and she nodded at them, her lips plastered with a benign smile. She went upstairs, into the room reserved for the ladies' necessities, and found herself alone.

At once she straightened her bent back and crooked shoulders. Her chin lifted, and she swept the spectacles from her face. Shoving black lace half mittens up to her wrists, old Miss Cowper vanished, and in her place stood Emily Fox, known to her friends as Emmie, to many a scoundrel as Mrs. Apple, to Society variously as Miss Cowper, Lady Jane Effingham, and Françoise Marie de Fontages, Comtesse de Rohan.

"Emmie Fox, you're a devil, tormenting that man," she muttered to herself.

She hadn't been able to resist taunting the marquess. He was vain, arrogant, and foul-tempered. With all his riches he was still dissatisfied with the world. He owned at least three houses she knew of, and yet he couldn't summon the graciousness to forbear with silly but well-meaning young ladies. The man even had a hidden treasure. She'd heard about it from her mother, who had been fond of relating stories of the aristocracy and their grand houses. Agincourt Hall, the North family seat, stood among the grandest, and tales were told of the secret cache of gold concealed there by an Elizabethan nobleman. A man with all those houses and a treasure, too, had little of which to complain.

However, Emmie had to admit her opinion of

most men was as low as the belly of a Thames water rat. And perhaps her opinion of the marquess was influenced by the way her blood seemed to go from simmer to boil in a heart's beat at the sight of him.

Emmie had met lots of handsome men, but North seemed to provoke attacks of quivering knees and face flushes in her for no reason. Why should she develop vapors at the sight of his cavalry officer's body and fierce gray eyes? His appealing mouth was always frowning, and he usually seemed about to explode into a tirade. So why did his presence send alternating chills and waves of heat whisking through her?

Emmie shook her head. "This is no time to start dithering about some pretty, blue-blooded toff. Be about your business, Emmie, my girl."

Thrusting her spectacles in a skirt pocket, Emmie hurried through a series of connecting rooms to the gallery that extended the length of the house. The North gallery was famous for its expanse of floor-to-ceiling windows and for the collection of paintings that covered the opposite wall. Emmie peeked around a door, ascertained that the place was deserted, and hurried down the gallery. Its recently installed gas candle sconces cast a low gold light interspersed with shadows. She could barely make out the largest paintings—a Botticelli, a Titian, and a Rubens—but she swept by them and stopped in front of a small portrait of Henry VIII's sister Mary, by Holbein.

Glancing around to make sure she was still alone, Emmie grabbed her skirts and crinoline and pulled them up so that she could reach the tools concealed in a bag suspended from her waist. She removed tape, glue, a knife, and a rolled piece of canvas. Her fingers moving with swift assurance, she whipped the portrait off the wall, turned it over, and cut it out of its frame. It was the work of less than five minutes for her to replace the picture with the forgery she'd brought with her.

The original was carefully slipped into a large pocket sewn into her petticoat. After concealing her tools once more, Emmie replaced the forgery on the wall. She stood back and eyed it to make sure it was straight. Satisfied, she whirled around and sped down the gallery. Before reappearing in the ladies' withdrawing room she replaced her spectacles and resumed her Miss Cowper posture. Next, she sent word through a maid to Lady Buxton and her hostess that fatigue required her to leave early.

Donning her cloak Emmie hobbled down the front stairs where Turnip was already waiting with her carriage. As the vehicle left the North grounds at a sedate pace, she drew the shades and fell back against the squabs. What a tiresome evening.

Emmie smiled to herself. Tiresome except for

the amusement of sparring with that dreadful marquess. Unfortunately, his faults didn't seem to prevent her from feeling a most disturbing attraction to the man. It was fortunate that she would never see him again.

It had been obvious from the moment she set eyes on the marquess that he thought his personal beauty, rank, and wealth relieved him of any obligation to be kind or courteous. She hated men who felt such an overblown sense of entitlement. She'd known too many like him, the most destructive and evil of which had been her stepfather, Edmund Cheap.

But she needn't think of him. He was dead. And he'd left her to cope with the consequences of his bad character—two stepbrothers and one stepsister left destitute and abandoned. She remembered her astonishment at discovering the children five years ago. Had it been that long already? Emmie smiled as she remembered. Yes, it had been that long because Sprout, the youngest, had been a babe. Flash, the oldest boy, had been five, and little Phoebe had been two.

Her stepfather had been keeping another woman in St. Giles, a woman more suited to his tastes than Emmie's gently born mother. Yet he'd done no better by this woman or her children. The mother had died shortly after Emmie's stepfather,

leaving the children to Emmie, who hadn't known
of the existence of this second family.

As the carriage rattled along the Strand, heading
east, it slowed and turned into a side street. When
it came to a halt Emmie pulled up the shade and
leaned out the window. A scrawny shadow detached itself from a group of loiterers and stepped
into the road.

"Good evening, Wombie."

"Evenin', Missus Apple."

Handing Wombie the painting, she waited only
to see the forger walk quickly away from the carriage. Two of her men joined him as escorts, and
they vanished beyond the light of a gas lamp. Emmie lowered the shade, and Turnip set the carriage
in motion again.

While she removed the white wig and makeup
that aged her fifty years, Emmie mentally counted
the funds she'd saved at her bank and added the
profits from this latest theft.

"Still not enough."

Anxiety returned like a small, filthy vulture to
sit on her shoulder and weigh upon her soul. Her
dear Flash, the oldest of her stepbrothers, would
soon reach the age at which he must be sent to
school. Emmie had promised herself that her siblings would not suffer the same fate she had. Emmie's mother, Miss Jane Margaret Fox, had been
an improverished gentleman's daughter, naive and

foolish. So foolish that she'd fallen prey to her employer's wiles immediately upon being hired as a governess. Her mother's gullibility still appalled Emmie.

To trust a man in such a way was not within Emmie's nature to comprehend. Shaking her head at the folly of it, Emmie wiped her face with a damp cloth from her makeup case. Of course Mother had been thrown into the streets once she'd conceived Emmie. If she hadn't met and married Edmund Cheap, who knows what would have happened to her?

But Cheap had been as bad as the so-called gentleman. He had been a swell mobsman, one of the thieves who preyed upon the wealthy. Of course, Jane Margaret hadn't realized Cheap's occupation at first. Eventually her husband's character revealed itself. Faced with the enormity of her mistake, Jane Margaret chose to ignore it, remaining a lady in every way possible and raising her daughter as one.

Unfortunately, after Emmie's mother died, Cheap's thieving skills deteriorated under the influence of drink. Emmie had been forced to live in more and more disreputable circumstances as her stepfather's fortunes plummeted. By the time she was thirteen, Emmie had to take care of herself. The skills of a lady, which her mother had so lovingly taught, wouldn't put food on the table in St.

Giles. Learning the art of thieving from Cheap's associates, Emmie had become one of the swell mob.

One of the few good turns Edmund Cheap ever did her was helping her invent Mrs. Apple. To protect her from the dangers of the East End she acquired a fictional husband, who was conveniently dead. Learning rapidly, she had gathered around her protectors and allies, so that now she commanded the loyalty of over a dozen skilled subordinates. Yes, she owed Mrs. Apple to Edmund Cheap. She also owed him her mother's death from grief and ill health brought on from living in the disease-ridden slum courts of London.

Never mind. Cheap and his two wives were gone, and Emmie was left to fend for herself and her little family. She might have to spend her life among thieves, pickpockets, and harlots, but neither Flash nor Phoebe nor Sprout would ever set foot in the rookeries again. Emmie would steal from the queen herself before she'd let that happen.

Now the children lived in Kensington in a lovely house surrounded by trees and gardens. Each would receive a proper upbringing and an education at the best schools, which would afford introductions to the right people. Respectable

people, not the swell mobsmen who filched ladies'
purses and ended in Newgate. Not climbing
boys who burgled houses, not mouchers who
scrounged for what they could get.

Not for her brothers and sister the thieves'
kitchens of east London, or the servants' lurks
where those who drank too much or stole from
their employers took refuge. Emmie was sick of
the dark labyrinths of the rookeries where traps
were laid for the police or the unwary. But until
she could get enough money together, places like
that would serve as her office, drawing room, and
bedchamber.

The carriage stopped on the outskirts of St.
Giles. Emmie got out on a corner where a woman
was selling meat pies to two men in threadbare
coats.

"Getcher 'ot pies! Hot'n'fresh."

Emmie looked up at her coachman. "Well
done, Turnip. Back to the stables with you."

"Yes, missus. Pleasant evening, missus."

Emmie turned to find the two men gulping
down the last of their meat pies. "Hello, Snoozer,
Sweep."

Her two bodyguards doffed their caps.

"We was getting worried, Missus Apple," said
Snoozer. He had the build of a navvy, one of the
thousands of railroad workers who plagued England with their rowdiness.

Sweep wasn't as burly as Snoozer, but he was much taller and got his name from his former profession as a chimney sweep. "We thought pr'aps that toff what you stole the picture from caught you."

"Now, Sweep, have I ever been caught?"

"No, Missus, but you never know when some cove'll peach on you."

"And risk your wrath?" Emmie replied with a grin.

Sweep rarely smiled, but his lips did curl a bit as they set out down the lane. It took them half an hour to reach Madame Rachel's Boarding House in Needle Street off Blackfriars, but Emmie was careful never to attract attention to herself by taking the carriage back to her rooms. In any case, it was necessary to go by a circuitous route to make sure they weren't followed.

Eventually Emmie was ensconced in her sitting room in the boardinghouse. It was filled with threadbare furniture bought secondhand, but it was clean. Above her were the rooms of Wombie the forger, and in the cellar Borgle, the most successful fence in London, plied his trade. By now he would be poring over the Holbein portrait. Once they settled on a price, Borgle would send it to a buyer in Holland.

Downing the last of her cup of tea, Emmie listened to the swish of tarlatan skirts that announced the arrival of her friend Dolly Quill. Dolly sailed into the room without knocking, her wide skirts swaying. Miss Quill was one of the swell mob who operated among the gentry, dressed well, and lived in a good house in west London.

"Well, there you are." Dolly tossed her bright yellow hair and sat down beside Emmie. "All safe and successful once again, I see. I declare, Emmie, you're the only woman I know who can keep company with smashers, coiners, and half-drunk hags and make a profit of it."

Emmie set her teacup in its saucer and sighed. "You know how I manage things, and it isn't by wasting my time with petty thieves."

Dolly patted her hand, and Emmie smiled. Dolly liked to tease; it was her way of showing an affection that began when Emmie had saved her from Newgate prison. One day a few years ago she'd opened her carriage door to Dolly and hidden her from the policemen chasing her for stealing a lady's shopping money.

Pouring herself a cup of tea, Dolly settled back in her chair and took a sip. "Fancy someone paying all that blunt for a moldy old picture."

Emmie didn't bother to explain the importance of the Tudor portrait or its painter. Educated by her mother, she had found her gentle upbringing both an advantage and a hindrance among the denizens of underworld London.

"You sure that marquess won't discover the switch tonight and come looking for you?"

"Why do you think I chose the Norths for this lay?" Emmie replied. "The marquess is known for his dislike of London and the Season. He won't be here for the whole of it, and he spends most of his time at his country house or abroad. While he is here, he'll be too busy with engagements to inspect the gallery." Emmie frowned as she recalled both the handsome marquess and her lack of funds.

"What's wrong, my dear?"

"It's not enough, Dolly. Flash must be sent to school—Eton or Harrow—next year. A governess is all very well for the younger ones, but Flash will be eleven next year. I can't wait any longer than that."

"Don't see why he's got to go at all."

Emmie pinched the bridge of her nose and squeezed her eyes shut. The worry was making her head ache.

"It's quite simple," she said. "Acquaintances and friendships formed at schools like that introduce a child to Society. Without them, Flash won't be able to pursue a respectable profession or make a suitable marriage."

Dolly leaned toward her and spoke gently. "And that's why you live two lives—one here and one with the children. So's they can be respectable."

"Without respectability and education they'll descend to slum courts and streets with open sewers running down the middle of them."

"Like you," Dolly said.

Emmie swallowed hard. "Like me."

They sat in silence for a while before Emmie began drumming her fingers on the arm of her chair. Dolly raised a brow.

"What're you planning now?"

"I need more money, quick." Emmie stopped drumming and tapped her front teeth with a fingernail. "Hmmm. Tonight's lay was so easy, I think I'll go back and have another try. I saw a good bit of silver lying around collecting dust."

Dolly shook her head until her curls came loose. "Don't! It's too dangerous."

"It isn't."

"What's got into you? You got a precious strange look in your eye, my girl."

"Nonsense. There's no danger, and besides, North deserves to be taught a lesson in humility. I'm just the one to do it."

"If you don't look sharp and control yourself, you're going to end up lagged." Dolly was watching Emmie closely. "This North, he's weighing on your mind. That's not like you."

"Valin North is spoiled, rude, arrogant, and self-ish."

"And pretty, from what I hear."

"He may be," Emmie said, "but he knows it. It was disgusting to watch him play the grand lord and turn his back on a girl simply because he wouldn't trouble himself to be patient with her. He thinks he's entitled to the cream of life and has the right to trod upon everyone's feelings."

"That's the same things you say about old Mr. Cheap. You're letting your feelings run your head. Leave North alone, my dear, or you'll end up in Newgate, or worse."

"Not me," Emmie said as she poured herself more tea. "I'm going to get the money I need and humble that odious Valin North at the same time. He can spare the blunt, and he can certainly spare a bit of his arrogance. I intend to see that he learns consideration and humility, and I won't do him a morsel of harm."

Dolly was looking at her with suspicion. "Why are you so bloody anxious to see this toff again if he's such an arse?"

"I'm not," Emmie exclaimed.

"Plenty of other blokes with valuables worth stealing."

"I already know the lay for this one."

"Never go back to the same place for your pickings," Dolly said. "It's a rule."

"But not a law."

Dolly rose, shaking her head again. "It's a rotten idea."

"Don't worry," Emmie said with a grin. "It will be a lark."

2

The next morning Emmie woke feeling sluggish from a night of disturbing dreams. That damned marquess had invaded her sleep. In the dream she, not the voluble Lady Millicent, had been introduced to him.

In the dream, he had scowled at her in that off-with-her-head manner of his, just as he had poor Lady Millicent. But in the dream she had widened her eyes in response, and his scowl vanished like mist blown by a gale.

Suddenly Valin North's face lost the hardness of a Cossack warrior. Without harshness, it was a face of near perfection with its high forehead, emphasized by dark hair swept back in long soft waves. In a man without that straight nose and gently curved mouth the severity of such a haircut would have exposed and emphasized any imperfections. But what attracted Emmie's attention, what caused her blood to pound in her temples, were his eyes. Light gray, deep-set, and provocative, they seemed to bore through her, searching, invading, and thrusting aside all resistance.

In her dream Emmie met that compelling gaze for an eternity before the marquess stretched out a hand. Just as he touched her she woke.

"Gracious mercy," she muttered to herself. "I've lost my wits."

She was sitting in her shabby-genteel sitting room at a small desk going over her accounts for the fifth time. Laying down her pen, Emmie sighed and pressed her palms to her closed eyes. She was irritated at herself for losing her concentration.

All morning her thoughts had strayed from business to the dream, to Valin North. She was growing more and more uneasy. In all her exploits, all her deceits, she'd never encountered a man who hadn't vanished from her memory the instant he was out of her sight. Perhaps she should heed Dolly's warning.

With resolution she harnessed her thoughts again. Her conclusion of last night had been correct. She desperately needed more money for Flash, Sprout, and Phoebe.

A knock at the door interrupted her fretting,

and Wombie the forger entered. Wombie was dressed as a clerk, in a black suit. When he wasn't speaking of business, he had a number of chronic ailments that made up the bulk of his conversation. Wombie had taken up forgery so that he needn't pursue more physically demanding work that would aggravate his complaints. He wore spectacles with bottle-glass lenses, and boasted a luxurious mop of gray hair.

Wombie pushed his spectacles up the bridge of his nose with one hand while he clutched a flat wooden box with the other. "Missus Apple, might I trouble you to keep your parcel in your rooms while I go out?"

"What's wrong?" Emmie rose and took the box from him.

"I am Suffering From My Head, this morning. It's giving me terrible trouble, and I got to go to the apothecary for headache powders afore I'm forced to take to me bed."

Wombie also Suffered From His Feet and From His Back in a never-ending cycle of affliction. "I'd leave it with my 'prentice, but he's copying a will what just come to us sudden-like."

"You should stop here and send your 'prentice for the powders."

"Thank you, missus, but the will's got to be done by tonight, and since I'm Suffering From My Head, the boy's got to do this piece of work."

When Wombie was gone, Emmie returned to her desk and set the box down. They were waiting for Borgle to ship the painting tonight, but the box hadn't been nailed shut yet so she took the opportunity to remove the painting. Since Wombie hadn't yet reframed it, she was able to lay the picture flat on the desk to admire it.

Hans Holbein the Younger had been a favorite artist of Henry VIII and one of the finest painters of his time. After the theft, Emmie hadn't had time to study the naturalism of this portrait of the king's sister Mary Tudor, whose dark-haired and pink-cheeked beauty seemed as fresh as the day it was painted over three hundred years ago.

"Three hundred years," Emmie murmured, suddenly aware of how fragile the portrait might be.

She picked it up gently, intending to replace it in the box, but she noticed that the top edge of the canvas was uneven. She touched a bit of material sticking out there, thinking she would have to call it to Wombie's attention. As her finger slid over the flaw Emmie frowned. The protrusion was sharp, like paper rather than canvas. She peered more closely, then turned the painting over and examined its edges.

There was an extra layer of backing that had been glued onto the back of the original. When she'd cut the painting out of its frame, she'd loosened it. What she was looking at was the corner of something stuck between the portrait and the backing.

Drumming her fingers on the desk, Emmie stared at the Holbein. One of her advantages over the ordinary villains of east London was her education. Mother had taught her more than simple reading and writing.

Emmie had learned history, literature, languages, and art. She'd tried to continue with some of her education on her own. Her education had enabled her to recognize the value of the Holbein and choose North as her victim. Mother had also taught her etiquette and the nuances of titles—and the stories of England's great families.

It was Mother who had told Emmie about the Norths and their great country house, Agincourt Hall, where a great treasure was said to have been hidden shortly before King Phillip of Spain sent the Armada against England's Queen Elizabeth. Agincourt Hall had been owned by the Beauforts then, a Catholic family who had secretly plotted with the Spanish against the Protestant Elizabeth. Fearing the discovery of their plans and the Spanish gold sent to finance them, Henry Beaufort was said to have hidden the treasure somewhere in the house. He was arrested for treason and died in the Tower before he could reveal what he'd done with the treasure.

That was the story. Everyone thought it false because Elizabeth's master spy, Throckmorton, had scoured Agincourt Hall looking for the gold and discovered nothing. As a child Emmie had loved the story, though, because it was so much like a fairy tale. After the evil Beauforts had been disgraced, good Queen Bess had given the title and lands to a loyal man—Valin North's ancestor.

This portrait might have been among the original Beaufort possessions left at Agincourt. Emmie's drumming fingers stilled. They drifted toward the paper sticking out of the canvas, grasped, and tugged. More paper came out, then stuck. It appeared that there was more than one piece of paper folded together. Emmie grabbed a letter opener and carefully separated the backing from the portrait until there was room to slide out a sealed packet.

There was nothing written on the outside of the packet, but there was an impression on the wax that held it shut. She could make out a swan with its wings held back-to-back; perhaps the heraldic emblem of the Beaufort family? With precision she slid the blade of the letter opener under the seal. She was able to open the packet without damaging the wax.

Slowly she unfolded the papers and anchored them to the desktop with her inkstand and a paperweight. Then she sat there staring in disappointment at the top sheet of paper. It was yellow with age and written in an archaic script, but she could make out most of the words. At the top of the paper was a poem, and below this had been written a household register, a list of the members of the household of Henry Beaufort, Marquess of Westfield.

"Humph." Odd how she kept picturing Beaufort. He looked exactly like Valin North.

Shaking her head, Emmie went on to the next piece of paper, but as she turned the top sheet over, she noticed more writing on the back. Evidently the poem and register had been written on the reverse of an old letter. The second sheet was just as uninteresting. Emmie's gaze traveled down a list of rooms assigned to each household member who resided in Agincourt Hall itself. Next came a paper consisting of a series of foreign phrases, such as a student might copy for a lesson. Some were in Latin, and some in French and English.

Emmie studied a Latin phrase with little interest. *Sic itur ad astra*. The papers were worthless.

"Drat." She pounded her fist on the desktop. "Serves you right for letting your imagination rule your reason, my girl."

With a sigh Emmie pressed her palms against her eyelids again, then began to gather the papers. The sheet with the poem on it caught her attention as she placed it on top of the other two.

"What odd phrasing," she muttered as she read
it again.

> *Tho mighty Harry perish,*
> *And stalwart castle decay,*
> *Brave Westfield conquers triumphant.*
> *Mote and knole, hearth and court remain,*
> *For God's labor we do perform*
> *'Gainst Satan's evil and baseborn tyrant.*
> *To cast out the heretic serpent,*
> *To avenge one to the true church born.*

"Henry, old cove, you were no poet." Emmie
read down the list of household members that had
been added below the poem. "You had a giant
household, I'll admit." She read the old names
with growing interest.

HOUSEHOLD REGISTER
At my Lord's Table

My Lord	*My Lady*
My Lady Margaret	*My Lady Isabella*
Mr. Beaufort	*Mr. Fort*
John Musgrave	*Peter Garrett*
Monsieur d'Or	

The list went on to those privileged to dine "in
the Parlour," immediately below my lord's table.

Next came "The Clerk's Table" at which sat the upper servants such as the clerks of the kitchen and the yeomen of the buttery and pantry. Lower servants sat at the "Long Table in the Hall"—grooms, farriers, falconers, and bird-catchers. There were other tables where lowly persons like "Diggory Dyer and Marfidy Snipt" dined.

Emmie's lips curled. "Diggory Dyer, Monsieur d'Or. Ha!"

She glanced at the letter on the reverse of the household register, put it down, and immediately picked it up again. The date was March 23, 1588, and it was addressed to Henry Beaufort from Ferdinand Guzman de Silva, secretary to the Spanish ambassador to England.

"Eighty-eight," Emmie whispered to herself. "Eighty-eight. That's the year of the Armada."

Swiftly she read the phrases. *"Arm yourself," "The fleet sails from Lisbon in May."*

"Hmm. It's no wonder he hid this."

She read the second letter, which was from Beaufort to de Silva detailing his preparations to rise against Queen Elizabeth. Emmie was about to lose interest in the contents when she read Henry Beaufort's last words: *"I have received the gold and will employ it well."*

"The gold." The words were a long sigh.

Letting the paper fall from her hands, Emmie stared at the two missives. The letters had been written first. That was obvious, for one didn't write to the Spanish ambassador's secretary on the back of a list of household room assignments, and certainly the secretary wouldn't have written his letter on something of Beaufort's. Which meant that someone had reused the letters. But Henry Beaufort would have concealed such treasonous correspondence, not given it to his servants to use as scrap paper.

"So Beaufort himself must have added the household register, the poem, and the foreign phrases. Why?"

Emmie looked at the additions again. It was a huge household, evidence of the marquess's great rank. He even had a Frenchman staying with him, Monsieur d'Or. Possibly a friend? Or a French tutor for the daughters, Lady Margaret and Lady Isabella.

Poor girls. While they were learning French with Monsieur d'Or, their idiot father was committing treason and getting himself thrown in the Tower. What happened to them and to poor Monsieur d'Or?

"D'Or." Emmie blinked at the name scrawled in ink with a quill, remembering Mother's French lessons.

"D'Or," she repeated as she stared at the household register. "*Un anneau d'or,* a gold ring. *Fil d'or,* gold thread. A French tutor named Master Gold. I think not."

With growing excitement Emmie looked at the poem that had been written on the back of the Spaniard's letter. It referred to casting out the heretic serpent to avenge one born of the true church, so these additions to the letters were from the time shortly before the Armada. And the Armada had been sent to avenge the death of the Catholic Mary, Queen of Scots, at the hands of Elizabeth. Mary Stewart had been born into the true church.

Henry Beaufort was recording something important, something he had to conceal—the Spanish gold, Monsieur d'Or. What of the room assignments on the back of Beaufort's letter? Everyone seemed to have ordinary rooms except Monsieur d'Or, who was lodged in *"la chambre sur la spirale,"* whatever that meant. "The room under the spiral"?

Shoving the Beaufort letter aside, Emmie examined the paper bearing the various phrases. The first phrase was in English, and Biblical: "For where your treasure is, there will your heart be also. Matthew 6:21."

"Poor Henry," Emmie said. "Did you really think to fool a man like Throckmorton or a queen like Elizabeth with such obvious ruses? It's amazing you weren't found out sooner."

It seemed that the only clever thing Beaufort

did was hide the papers. Something here must tell the location of the gold!

Emmie dropped the paper, jumped up, and began pacing. She would have to translate the foreign phrases. She'd need those old Latin and French dictionaries of her mother's. She halted in midstride.

"Gracious mercy, all that blunt hid in North's house, and I can't get to it." She rubbed her forehead. "Humbling the marquess will have to wait."

She resumed her march around the sitting room, passing the couch with its patched upholstery concealed by pillows. "I must get into Agincourt Hall by some handy means."

She could go as Agnes Cowper, but it would be hard to maneuver as an old lady in a place as large as Agincourt. A disguise as a parlor maid would be easy enough, but a servant's time wasn't her own. Her movements would be hampered by supervision from the butler and housekeeper, and she would have to work from dawn until late at night.

No, the best choice was to go as a young lady. Forbidden by convention from pursuing many activities and professions open to men, young women of breeding had abundant time on their hands.

"Just the thing," Emmie said. She plopped down on the sofa and tapped her front teeth with her fingernail. "Who shall I be?"

A few moments later she clapped her hands and stood, her eyes gleaming as she announced to the sitting room, "Valin North, prepare to meet Miss Emily Charlotte de Winter. Whether you like it or not, your aunt is going to invite her to Agincourt Hall for a long, long visit."

3

A fugitive in his own home, Valin tiptoed past the top of the staircase with his collie, Megan, right behind him. He paused to listen to his aunt's squalling.

"Thistlethwayte? Thi—stle—thwayte! These flowers are wilting, and the guests haven't even arrived. Thistlethwayte!"

This last cry was more of a screech. Valin winced, and Megan ducked her head and gave a soft moan.

"Come on, girl."

He sped along the landing to the east wing. He could hear Megan's nails clicking on the floor as he crept past his own rooms and around a corner. Slipping through a door, he entered the book-lined chamber he'd made into his study. Valin shut the door while Megan trotted over to the fireplace and curled up on the large embroidered cushion reserved for her. Valin turned the key in the lock, sighed, and smiled at the collie.

"We'll get a bit of peace in here, girl. Can't hear Aunt at all."

Unbuttoning his evening coat, Valin estimated he had almost an hour before he had to receive the guests who'd been invited to Ottoline's ball. This evening's entertainment was yet another attempt to match him with a suitable young lady. Aunt wasn't about to give up, and Valin had resigned himself to the necessity of marrying. He'd avoided it for years, but he was thirty-one, and it was time.

Still, he couldn't help being resentful. He wouldn't have to marry at all if his brothers weren't so unsatisfactory. If Acton were to inherit, he'd ruin the estates in a year with his debts, and poor Courtland was so caught up in his research he barely remembered what month it was. If a subject had nothing to do with his medieval studies, it wouldn't hold Courtland's attention for more than two minutes.

Had either of his brothers showed the talent or inclination to manage the vast North holdings, Valin would have remained single. It was all he was fit for—solitude. Now he would have to find a young woman he could tolerate. Once married, he'd spend his life dreading that his wife might discover the secret he'd kept so long.

Valin closed his eyes as images forced themselves upon him. Flames, twisting, jumping flames. The heat blistering wood, baking brick. Timbers snapping and crashing as the roof of the old lodge collapsed. He could feel his skin burn as he stood on the lawn and watched hell's destruction overtake his father and his stepmother. He could see their writhing figures—black silhouettes that danced before the windows.

Something touched his leg, jolting Valin out of the nightmare. He glanced down to find Megan tapping him with her paw. Her ears pricked, and he knelt to stroke her.

"Thanks, Meggie. You're a good girl. I'll look at my letters, shall I?"

He went to the deep leather wing-back chair behind his desk. His secretary had left the mail, and Valin began to read through it. He served on a committee with Miss Nightingale and Mr. Gladstone, Chancellor of the Exchequer. They were working to provide employment for veterans of the Crimean War, care for the permanently disabled, and support and education for the war widows and orphans. There were too many men with arms and legs blown away. Too many women who had never buried their husbands because the Russian cannons had left nothing to send home.

Valin worked for a few minutes, then turned his attention to a scheme to educate and place scientifically trained nurses in hospitals. He was cursing the backwardness of the old medical establishment when his secretary, Wycliffe Leslie, knocked and asked to be admitted. Valin opened the door. With a wooden expression, Mr. Leslie held out a thick envelope. His manner sent a chill of warning through Valin as he accepted the envelope.

"Thank you, Leslie. What is it?"

Mr. Leslie cleared his throat. "Items given to me by Lord Acton, which he wishes to bring to your attention immediately, sir."

Refraining from expressing his true feelings, Valin thanked his secretary and dismissed him. He shut the door and leaned against it while he glared at the envelope.

"Hell and damnation. Not again."

Inside the packet, Valin found almost a dozen markers, debts his brother owed from horse racing and gambling. "Bloody hell and damnation!"

The door rattled against his back. Whirling around, Valin yanked it open. Acton stood with his hand raised to knock.

"Damnation, Acton."

His brother held out a folded piece of paper. "I forgot this one."

Valin rolled his eyes without taking the paper and stood aside. "Come in."

"Got to dress for the ball, old man."

"I said come in."

With a nonchalant air, Acton strolled into the study and rested a hip on Valin's desk. Valin stalked toward him, plucked the debt from Acton's fingers, and read it. Looking up slowly, he stared at his brother. Then he dropped the pile of notes on the desktop and went to the window. He brushed aside a heavy velvet curtain and stared at the darkened garden.

Without turning around, he said, "You realize, of course, that you've managed to waste half your yearly allowance, and it's only April."

"If you weren't such a miser, I wouldn't be caught short," Acton said lightly.

Valin concealed the hurt this response caused him. It never did to reveal one's feelings to Acton. "You get exactly what Father provided, and I give you additional funds."

"A pittance compared to what you have."

Valin released the curtain and faced his brother. "I've told you over and over, the income from the North estates is large, but it goes to maintain the houses, the lands, the servants and tenants."

"And the beggars and loose women you call veterans and nurses," Acton said with a bitter smile.

"I'll not deprive men of bravery and honor because you waste money playing Ecarte and All

Fours. If you can't control yourself, don't play cards. If you can't pick a winning horse, don't place bets."

Acton's air of insouciance vanished. He swore and banged his fist on the desk. "Why should I live like a pauper just because I was born three years later than you? It's not fair, by God. Everyone thinks I'd make a better marquess than you. I'm generous and open and easy to talk to. All you do is hide at Agincourt Hall and scowl and yell at everyone."

"There's more to a title than waving and bowing, Acton." Valin kept his feelings in check as he planted his hands on the desk and leaned toward his brother. "All you think about are the luxuries and privileges of rank, not the responsibilities and damned hard work that go with them."

"Ha!" Acton strutted to the door. "Are you going to pay those or not?"

Valin's shoulders drooped, and he turned away. "I'll pay them."

"I think it's the least you can do." Acton left, slamming the door behind him.

Feeling himself descend into the wasteland of misery Acton knew how to invoke so well, Valin wandered over to Megan and knelt to stroke her silky fur. He never wanted to fight with Acton. The younger man had suffered when they were children. While their father had browbeaten, criticized, and scolded Valin for his imperfections and treated Courtland as a genius whose eccentricities should be indulged, he'd ignored Acton. Neither the heir nor the genius, neither the hope for the future nor the youngest child, the old marquess had found Acton uninteresting.

Valin considered this neglect surprising, since it had been Acton who shared their father's interests—riding, hunting, shooting, gambling, clubs, the London Season, loose women. Acton had nearly ridden himself to death trying to impress the marquess with his equestrian prowess. It had been left to Valin to provide the admiration and attention Acton craved.

Valin rubbed his cheek against the top of the collie's head. "Is it my fault he's so spoiled, Megan?" The dog licked the back of his hand. "You think so? Well, you're usually right, but Mother was dead. Who else was there to—"

"Valin?" The door opened again to reveal a stack of books with legs.

"Come in, Courtland." Valin jumped up and grabbed some of the books as they threatened to spill to the floor.

"Thanks." Courtland was out of breath. He dropped into the wing-back chair in front of the desk and set his load of heavy tomes on his lap. "I'm glad I found you."

"You're not dressed," Valin said, placing the volumes he had rescued on the floor.

"No, I'm not," Courtland replied as he rummaged through a folder of papers on top of the books.

"Courtland."

"I know I put it in here."

"Courtland."

"I distinctly remember putting it in here, because I knew you'd want to see it."

"Courtland!"

His brother looked up, startled. "What?"

"You're not dressed."

"For what?"

"The ball," Valin said, knowing what question would be next.

"What ball?"

"The one Aunt is giving tonight that you promised to attend."

"Did I? I don't remember. Who cares about a ball, when I could have this!" With a flourish Courtland produced a piece of paper.

Valin took it, glanced at it, and raised his brows. "Just explain, Courtland."

"This will explain." Courtland set his books and papers aside, retrieved another sheet, and showed it to Valin. "This is a description of a chest containing dozens and dozens of rolls of arms. I found it in an old shop off the Strand."

"Yes," Valin said politely.

Courtland gave him a look of exasperation. "I examined them yesterday." Courtland's voice became hushed with awe. "They're all from one visitation of a herald in the sixteenth century under Henry VII, I think. This is only a partial list of what's in the chest—the roll of arms of the lord of the manor of Long Melford Hall in Suffolk, the Carlisle Roll, tournament rolls, grants of arms, illustrations of achievements."

"I see," Valin said. He didn't really, but there was no one else in the family who cared about Courtland's medieval studies.

Bending over, Courtland dropped the paper he was holding. It sailed past Megan to land under the desk, as he shuffled through his folder and grabbed another sheet.

"Here it is. Look at this, Valin." Courtland pointed to an illuminated drawing of coats of arms. "This one is the Moore achievement—Argent between three moorcocks and a chevron sable, and this is Langton—per pale azure and gules overall a bend Or."

Valin groaned at last. "You know I've forgotten most of those terms of heraldry. Stop talking like Clarenceaux, King of Arms."

"Valin, I think this chest holds some of the oldest records of arms ever discovered." Courtland lowered his voice in reverence again. "Do you know how rare such a find is? And I didn't look at the things in the bottom of the chest for fear the shopkeeper would realize how interested I was."

"And now you want to buy it," Valin finished for him.

Clutching his papers to his chest, Courtland swallowed and nodded.

"Why don't you?"

"The shopkeeper may not know the historical significance of the contents, but he knows they're old. He wants quite a bit for the lot."

Valin glanced at the quotation sheet in his hand again and whistled.

Courtland swallowed hard. "Too much?"

Noting his younger brother's pale complexion and the way his hands crumpled the papers they still held, Valin sighed and shook his head. Among their fellow English aristocrats for whom sport was the measure of a man, Courtland had suffered derision and isolation for his scholarly interests. He'd been beaten up at university more than once.

"I'll write you a cheque."

Papers flew in all directions as Courtland rushed at him. Valin found himself enveloped in a brief but violent hug.

"I knew you'd understand!"

"Of course," Valin said as he ruffled his

brother's hair. "You've made a priceless discovery. Just don't let the shopkeeper know before you've got the bill of sale in your hand."

Grinning, Courtland began gathering his books and papers. "I won't."

When his brother was gone, Valin settled in a chair by the fire to read a letter from the queen's foreign secretary, Lord John Russell. His hand dropped to stroke Megan, then flinched when a harpylike voice screeched at him.

"Valin, I know you're in there." Ottoline banged on the door. "The guests have been arriving for ten minutes, and if you don't come down and receive, my nerves will suffer a fatal crisis. I feel faint already."

Megan stuck her head under his chair as Valin rose and opened the door. Ottoline stood on the threshold in yards of pale pink satin more suitable to a girl than a widow. Valin suppressed a smile. Aunt had a good heart and she'd been a second mother to him after his own had died, but she made herself comical. With her short stature, wide face and shoulders, and large, protruding brown eyes, she resembled a King Charles spaniel.

Quivering so that the jewels at her neck and on her arms glittered, Ottoline bleated, "Why must you make me suffer so? Have I not done my best as your hostess after you asked me for help? No one understands my torment." Her voice changed to the crackle and snap of a master sergeant. "And Thistlethwayte has informed me you're leaving for Agincourt Hall before the end of May. The end of May, when the Season is at its height. You can't do this to me. I swear you'll drive me into a brain fever. Why did you ask me to help you find a suitable wife, if you were going to thwart me in all I try to accomplish?"

Ottoline's complaints showered over him as Valin turned and whistled to Megan. "Go to Mr. Leslie, girl. Time for your walk."

The collie was a streak of gold and white. Paws scrambling on the polished wood floor, she hurtled by Ottoline and down the hall. Wishing he could go with her, Valin offered his arm to his aunt and descended to the great marble-and-gilt entrance hall.

Half an hour passed while he greeted guests with such august and ancient names as Howard, Grey, Spencer, and Seymour. It was all he could do to clamp his jaw shut so that he didn't yawn. Now he was listening to the uninspired and insipid compliments of the lovely Miss Adelaide Beresford, who offered her most fascinating comment so far.

"I do so admire your floral arrangements, my lord. Using flowers as decoration is so festive."

Valin's stupor evaporated at the sound of a throaty feminine voice that cut through the drone of the crowd and the music.

"Indeed, Miss Beresford. How unusual to see flowers at a ball. But I think his lordship would prefer a more poetic expression. 'The summer's flower is to the summer sweet,/ Though to itself it only live and die.' "

While Adelaide gave a murmur of incomprehension, Valin turned to welcome the only person in years whose conversation might not make him wish to put a gun to his head rather than listen. His artificial smile faded as he met the forthright gaze of a young woman whose manner surprised and delighted him. Unlike most, she met his eyes without blushing, simpering, looking at his boots, or flapping her fan as though she were doing an Oriental dance.

"Oh, I am remiss," Adelaide said. "Valin North, may I present the honorable Miss Emily Charlotte de Winter. Miss de Winter is the great-niece of Miss Cowper, come home from school in France."

Valin bowed, his gaze taking in auburn hair, emerald eyes above a small straight nose, and a figure the stance of which reminded him of a grenadier on parade. Except for the curves, which immediately forced him to revise the image. Miss de Winter wasn't a great beauty—she wasn't as rounded or as pale as she should be for that—but the whole of her person fascinated despite this disadvantage. He lifted his eyes to those of his guest to find her watching him with detached amusement.

Another surprise. Few young ladies met him with such an attitude of equality and lack of feminine calculation. Although fawning admiration disgusted him, Valin found himself growing a bit irritated that this young lady excepted herself from the rest. As he straightened from his bow, he noticed that she curtsied in an offhand manner, as though it were an afterthought. Why did she not make this gesture a display of her grace, as did the other eligible girls introduced to him? Surely she knew he was available. And why was she smiling at him as though she knew what he was going to say next?

"You were at school in France, Miss de Winter?"

"Yes, my lord. A prejudice of my mother, who was finished there as well. But now I'm come home to be shown off and married off."

"Emily!" Adelaide was blushing and shushing her friend.

Miss de Winter shrugged, another gesture an English girl would avoid. "Everyone knows it. I might as well say it." She turned to Valin with a wry smile. "So much more efficient than speaking of the weather, which is horrid dull, don't you think?"

"I'm beginning to, Miss de Winter."

Before he'd spoken she moved down the receiving line, not at all bothered that the next girl and her parents had dislodged her from the place opposite him. While he engaged in yet another inane welcome, he watched Miss de Winter out of the corner of his eye. She was listening with sympathy to his aunt's complaints about the crush of people.

What was it about her? Even her dress was different, perhaps because it was French. That was part of it. She wasn't dressed in delicate pink, white, or ivory. Miss de Winter wore a rose-patterned silk gown of chestnut and bronze green. There were ivory roses in her swept-back hair and on her left shoulder, and the skirt of her gown was shaped differently, like a cone with a train that revealed yards and yards of luxurious, shimmering fabric.

He would never have noticed such details had he not spent the last tedious weeks listening to the conversation of young ladies. But thanks to his ordeal, he was able to recognize the work of Charles Frederick Worth of Paris. He remembered his aunt remarking that Worth spent time with his clients and designed a wardrobe that fit their personalities. Evidently Miss de Winter was dramatic, bold, and original.

As he bowed to his next guest, Valin murmured to himself, "Take heed, Miss de Winter. I'm going to find out if you're as fascinating as Mr. Worth would have everyone believe."

4

Valin North wasn't the fool Emmie had hoped he'd be.

To make things worse, his mere physical presence was interfering with the proper workings of her mind. To her dismay a part of herself she never knew woke, sat up, and paid bright, ear-pricked attention to Valin North—his horseman's body, gleaming mahogany hair, and wide mouth. This was a man who, despite his threatening, scowling manner, could have been a model for a sculptor or for a knight of the round table.

Nodding politely to indicate her interest in a boring conversation, Emmie scolded herself for losing sight of her goal—all because of a pretty man. She'd spent weeks preparing for this ruse, studying his reputation, learning about the family, their friends, and their servants. It had taken awhile to prepare her own character, to devise a history, to find a suitable wardrobe, and to find a gullible Society matron to serve as her sponsor.

Emmie stood beside the Society matron, Adelaide's mother, doing her best not to look at the marquess. It shouldn't be this hard not to look at him. Never had she encountered this urge to stare at a victim of one of her plots. She would not look at him. She wouldn't.

Even as she repeated these words to herself her gaze slid sideways to the tall figure striding across the dance floor to open the ball with the traditional quadrille. Who was he dancing with? The lady guest of the highest rank, of course, some dowager countess or duchess.

No, he wasn't a fool. Valin North had responded immediately to her quotation. He liked literature; she'd discovered that in her inquiries. It never did to embark upon a scheme such as this without knowing something of one's enemy. But no amount of inquiry could have prepared her for North's personal charm.

Her mouth had almost dropped open when he turned his gaze on her. For once he wasn't scowling, and those eyes had captured her attention at once. They were light gray, the color of a storm cloud lit from behind by white sunlight, the color of sunbeams reflecting on water.

Once she'd considered gray an ugly color. . . . Emmie came to herself with a jolt. What was she thinking? Gracious mercy, she would soon be fawning over him like all the other women.

Forcing her thoughts from the marquess, Emmie busied herself with the business of dancing. Soon she had written names on most of the ivory spokes of her fan, as her mother had described when she was little. However, her most important task was to ingratiate herself with North's Aunt Ottoline, the dowager Countess of Pomfret.

As his hostess, Lady Ottoline controlled access to the marquess, his social calendar, and most important, his guest list. While couples whirled on the dance floor and the chandeliers dripped candle wax on everyone, Emmie worked her way through a forest of crinolines, lace, and black evening coats to Ottoline's side.

"Oh, Miss de Winter, shall I find you a partner?" asked Lady Ottoline.

Emmie fluttered her fan and smiled. "I thank you, but this is the only time I've had to rest since I arrived. Lord Mimsey said you were a most accomplished hostess, but his compliments hardly did you justice, Lady Ottoline. Neither Devonshire House nor Chesterfield House can compare with North House."

"How sweet of you, my dear, but what it has cost my nerves no one can know."

"I'm so sorry," Emmie said with a sympathetic frown. "It must be difficult."

"Truly, my dear, it is. The guest list alone was a nightmare. I declare I had to consult DeBrett's at least a hundred times to get the seating right for supper. And this floor! The beeswax had gone bad . . ."

Emmie smiled and nodded, frowned and nodded, tut-tutted with compassion, and generally behaved as if Lady Ottoline's trials were the equivalent of those of Job. She was well rewarded. After a lengthy description of her troubles with her nerves and the vapors, Ottoline placed her gloved hand on Emmie's arm and gave her a smile.

"You're such a good girl. Not flighty and uncivil like so many young people today. I shall send my card to you, and you must return yours. You're staying with Adelaide?"

Emmie, in her guise as Miss Cowper, had written herself an introduction to Adelaide and was indeed staying with her. Expressing her deepest gratitude, Emmie allowed herself to be escorted to the dance floor by her next partner. The most delicate part of her task this evening had been accomplished.

She couldn't pursue the Norths' acquaintance unless Lady Ottoline called on her first. Now that the older woman was to send her carriage with a maid to present her card, this would establish Emmie as a member of the family's circle—those persons of rank, reputation, and civility with whom the marquess socialized.

Twirling around the room in the arms of a young man with a store of the fatuous conversation appropriate for debutantes, Emmie caught a glimpse of the marquess. He turned his partner in a circle and looked in Emmie's direction. Emmie gave her young man a glittering smile and laughed, even though he hadn't said anything funny.

She was disgusted that she felt an urge to impress Valin North—not just in order to gain access to his house and its hidden treasure, but to gain his admiration. She wanted to fascinate him as he was fascinating her. Why was she so obsessed?

Was it because, when he wished, he had exquisite manners that matched the elegance of his appearance? It couldn't be. She wasn't a dithering light-minded miss whose heart fluttered just because Valin North was at once inviting and dangerous.

She was Mrs. Apple, the leader of as disreputable a gang of villains as ever roamed the streets of St. Giles or Whitechapel. It was she who was dangerous.

Then why did her hands grow cold just looking at him?

"Gracious mercy, behave yourself," she mut-

tered as the dance ended. It was all she could do
not to look around in search of him.

"This is torture."

"I beg your pardon, Miss de Winter?" said her
partner.

"Oh, I said this is a pleasure. Such lovely music."

She spent the next three hours proving to herself that she could be in the same room with Valin
North and not look at him. During that time she
sensed his brooding regard more than once. Her
plan was working, then.

Once she had discovered a way to get herself to
this ball, Emmie had thought long about how to
attract the interest of so sought-after a man. Her
deliberations led her to the conclusion that indif-
ference would set her apart from the bleating herd
of debutantes that surrounded him. Men always
seemed to want what was beyond their reach.

The supper hour passed with Emmie snaring
the attentions of the heirs of a baron and an earl
and the rich younger son of a duke. The dances
after supper passed in a blur except when she spied
the marquess headed her way. This happened after
the second waltz.

Valin North had escorted his partner back to her
chaperone, turned smoothly, and walked straight
toward her. Emmie had nodded at the earl's son
like a queen to a courtier and slipped into the

crowd. Before the marquess could catch her, she went upstairs to the ladies' retiring room and spent a good quarter hour pretending to adjust her costume. By the time she returned to the ballroom North's famous scowl was back.

At last there were only a polka and two waltzes left in the evening. It was time. She danced the polka with the duke's son and at the end fluttered her fan and protested her fatigue. She sent her partner off in search of lemonade, then whirled in a cloud of bronze skirts and darted into the crowds around the dance floor.

Her path took her near enough to the marquess so that he couldn't help seeing her flee. With the air of one escaping unwanted attentions, Emmie sought the refuge of a screen and potted plants beside the soaring French doors that led to one of the balconies. A leaf tickled her shoulder and she swatted at it with her fan.

The etiquette Mother taught had been a useless accomplishment in the rookeries, but had become a boon now. One of its most important precepts was that young ladies at social functions did not seek out private places such as libraries or conservatories. A balcony was as intimate a setting as she was going to manage. Not that she wished to be alone with Valin North for long. Of course she didn't.

Emmie risked a glimpse between the leaves of

the ferns. Her heart bounced polkalike in her chest; he was only a couple of yards away! Despite the fact that she'd planned this encounter Emmie panicked, bolted, and nearly tripped over her skirts as she rushed around the screen and onto the balcony. Where once cool reason dwelt, confusion ruled, and Emmie struggled with a rush of feelings she didn't understand. All she knew was that Valin North made her insides quiver, and that she desperately wanted him to come to her while at the same time she dreaded it. As she tried to take herself in hand his voice cut through her thoughts and made her jump.

"Miss de Winter, are you well? Has the dancing wearied you?"

Emmie glanced over her shoulder at him, met those cloud-with-a-silver-lining eyes, and blurted out, "Oh, I rub on as well as I can."

"What?"

She could have bitten her lip. What a time for her to slip into thieves' cant. If she didn't take care, she'd be nattering about coiners, mouchers, and flash pubs.

"I'm quite well, thank you, my lord. I'm afraid I've danced with as many condescending young fops as I can manage this evening."

He was beside her, and she could feel the warmth of his body even across the two feet that separated them.

"Indeed," Valin said softly.

He looked down at her with a half smile of gentle amusement she'd never seen before. She looked away, out at the dark garden. Feeling heat rise from her neck to her face, she took refuge in one of her prepared speeches.

"I love such nights in early spring, the chill with a promise of warmth to come, but I'm afraid the mists are rising, and that always reminds me of *Macbeth*."

"Macbeth," came the startled response.

"Oh, yes. You know, 'Double, double toil and trouble;/ Fire, burn; and, caldron, bubble.' "

"Good God, she's read a book."

"I beg your pardon?"

"Forgive me. I should have said, good God, she's read something other than a novel."

Emmie curled her lip at the note of arrogant surprise in his voice. To think she'd wanted this man's company just moments ago. How she detested the pride and ignorance of men, especially aristocrats. Those old feelings of resentment provoked instant, explosive anger and overcame her good sense. Valin North was most irritating.

"What an ignorant assumption, my lord, that all women are unread. Allow me to provide you with further proof of your mistake."

She planted her fists on her hips and kicked her train aside. " 'Fillet of a fenny snake,/ In the caldron boil and bake.' " She advanced on North, making him back away from her as she chanted, " 'Eye of newt, and toe of frog,/ Wool of bat, and tongue of dog.' "

His eyes widened when her gaze held his without faltering. " 'Adder's fork, and blind-worm's sting,/ Lizard's leg, and howlet's wing.' " She took another step; he kept backing up. Emmie raised her voice and stuck out her chin. " 'For a charm of pow'rful trouble,/ Like a hell-broth boil and bubble.' " Valin North bumped ignominiously against the stone balustrade.

Noting the astonished look in his eyes, she turned her back on her host and sauntered inside. "Good evening to you, my lord."

As she left she heard him whisper, "Damn."

She was almost through the balcony doors when a gloved hand fastened around her arm and swung her around. North pulled her into the shadows of the balcony with a chuckle.

"How easily you take offense."

Emmie jerked her arm free. "How easily you give it, my lord." She moved toward the doors again, but he put his arm out to stop her.

"Don't go. You can't blame me for being surprised."

He had moved closer, but it was so dark she could see only the line of his cheek and the brilliant white of his shirt. She had already allowed him to stand there too long. Ladies kept a distance from gentlemen.

Emmie edged a step away from him. "I do blame you. All women are not the same."

"No, they're not, and you've proved it tonight. Will you honor me with this next waltz?"

"I believe Adelaide and her mother are leaving."

North offered his arm. "They can't leave without you, and you will be dancing the last waltz with me. Come, Miss de Winter. It will be your triumph."

"It will? Why?"

At this, North stared at her in a puzzled manner. "Surely you know the marriage market game. You said you were here to be shown off and married off."

"Those are my family's plans, my lord. It does not follow that they're also mine."

There. She had regained mastery of herself. A short silence ensued during which Emmie calmly adjusted her gloves.

"Dear God, you mean it."

"I mean it, or I wouldn't have said it, and since we're being familiar, my lord, I'll tell you this. I'm not marrying a fool or a wastrel or anyone distasteful to me simply to be married. I'd rather be alone than spend my life in respectable misery."

North slapped the balustrade and uttered a sharp laugh that made Emmie jump.

"Upon my word, you're the first young lady I've ever met with conversation of substance and an honest and forthright manner. Is this the result of French boarding school?"

His grin softened the severity of his face, and Emmie smiled. "I think it's the result of my own obstinate character." She turned to go. "Now, if you will excuse me, I've been forthright enough for one evening."

"Then you won't waltz with me."

"Haven't you danced enough with simpering young ladies and ambitious mamas?"

"But you just said you're not ambitious."

"I'm not, and I shan't remain on this balcony with you any longer, my lord."

"Ha!" North swiftly stepped in her way. "So you do fear Society's censure."

"I know what honor requires of me, my lord."

"Honor. What a tiresome word," North said softly.

It was the rough quality of his voice that alarmed her. He caught her gloved hand and kissed it before she could protest. Then, without her understanding how it happened, she had backed against the balustrade, and he was much too close. A dark shadow against the lights of the ballroom, he seemed to grow taller than his already substantial height. Confusion descended upon her once more, and she began to feel most odd.

He was moving again! If she wasn't careful, he would touch her, and then something dreadful would happen. Her wobbly knees might give way. To stop him she began to chatter.

"A lady's honor is never tiresome—"

Words stuck in her throat when North ignored her and touched the backs of his fingers to her cheek.

"Forget about tiresome propriety," he whispered. "Your honesty and frankness are more fascinating than the greatest beauty."

His breath in her ear caused exotic feelings to erupt in her body. Emmie dropped her fan. He wasn't supposed to try to seduce her! Where were her audacity and courage? She was known in the rookeries for her audacity and courage.

Feeling herself begin to tremble under his touch, Emmie blurted out, "One's good name is beyond price." He only smiled and bent down, his lips parted. Emmie gasped, dashed sideways, and rounded on him.

"Drat if I'll allow you to ruin my good name for a whim, my lord marquess."

Leaning against the balustrade, North gave her a mocking smile and said quietly, "I felt you trembling, Emily Charlotte de Winter."

"That's quite enough liberty of conversation,"

Emmie said. She whirled around and marched to the doors, but stopped to glare at him over her shoulder. "I may not want to get married, but I'm not a fool. '. . . He that filches from me my good name/ Robs me of that which not enriches him,/ And makes me poor indeed.' And it's I who will suffer from its lack, not you."

"You can't hide behind quotations forever."

"Good evening to you, my lord." The heels of her slippers tapped loudly on the marble floor as she stamped away.

"Good evening, my lady coward."

Emmie kept walking and didn't look back. She was sitting beside Adelaide in the carriage as it drove away before she realized she'd forgotten to pick up her fan.

5

It was three o'clock in the morning, the last of his guests had gone, and Valin couldn't sleep. At first he'd blamed his worries: the struggle to promote properly trained nurses, the Crimean widows and orphans, and most of all, Acton. If unchecked, Acton could get himself so deeply in debt that Valin's cherished projects would suffer. And by God, no spoiled young wastrel was going to deprive the suffering of help.

But such cares weren't what kept him awake. A throaty voice, green eyes, and auburn hair kept him awake. Emily de Winter's mouth with its short upper lip and full lower one kept him awake. Valin stretched out his hand to touch the rosewood box on the table beside his bed. He'd put her fan in it. He was making himself ridiculous, keeping a lady's fan. It was something spotty-faced youths did.

Valin turned on his side and breathed a sigh. Wakeful nights had been his curse for years after the fire that had killed his father and Carolina. He thought he'd made peace with himself about their deaths, but lately the old nightmare had returned. Now Miss de Winter threatened his slumber, too.

Miss de Winter was different. For one thing, she was more sure of herself than a girl sheltered in a boarding school should have been. She behaved toward him with the confidence of a woman twice her age. Such poise in an eligible young lady was unheard-of—and it was fascinating because she couldn't be more than twenty.

She had malachite green eyes. . . .

Valin sat up in bed. Uttering a wordless sound of disgust, he threw back the covers and got out of bed. The room was dark, made more so by the burgundy damask curtains drawn over the windows. Valin thrust the heavy material aside and looked outside. The garden was still quite dark, but dawn wasn't far away, because there was enough light to see the gravel paths between the apple trees his grandfather had planted. He laid his forehead against the pane and took a deep breath.

"Valin North, get hold of yourself." He had to take the very rich and pretty Miss Philippa Kingsley riding early this morning. He groaned at the thought. Another callow young lady.

He'd much rather go riding with Emily de Winter. God forgive him, what he really wanted to do with Emily wasn't to be thought of. He hadn't known how utterly miserable he'd been until he met her. He'd been living in a nightmare because he was surrounded by people whose interest in Society he didn't share. God, he'd wager boredom could be fatal, to the spirit at least. And then Emily de Winter had quoted Shakespeare at him.

The summer's flower is to the summer sweet, / Though to itself it only live and die.

She was like that, a summer flower come to grace his barren garden. Valin lifted his head from the windowpane. "Dear God, what am I thinking? I'm waxing poetic about a young lady I barely know."

And there was something strange about Miss de Winter. Not just her air of assurance, but something more. He couldn't quite decide what it was. Perhaps it was her foreign upbringing, although she didn't have an accent. A young woman raised mostly in France should have an accent. And then there was the way she'd suddenly appeared in Society out of nowhere. Few people knew her. He'd asked around. There was something mysterious about Emily de Winter. Thank Providence. Here was someone who interested him, intrigued him, and made him feel alive among Society's dead fish.

He wanted to solve the mystery of Emily de Winter. Damn! He was mooning over a woman. He never lost sleep over women. They'd fallen into his arms too often for that. This lady intrigued him, but he wouldn't make a fool of himself over her.

Yanking the curtain back into place, Valin stomped back to bed. He jerked the covers over his head, annoyed with himself and determined to forget Miss Emily de Winter. At least for now. He had to get some sleep; he could think about her all he wanted in the morning. Then it occurred to him that he didn't know when he'd see her again. Surely he would see her again. She'd said she was in town to be married off.

Sighing, Valin sat up and rubbed his burning eyes. He'd have to see her again. Perhaps next time she wouldn't seem so fascinating or mysterious, and then he could forget about her and get some blasted sleep.

❧

Emmie—alias Mrs. Apple or Miss Emily Charlotte de Winter—was invited to Agincourt Hall, as she'd intended from the moment she discovered the clues to the hiding place of the Spanish gold.

The intervening weeks were barely long enough for her to find a suitable chaperone and a girl who knew enough about the job to be her lady's maid.

Emmie located a Society matron who, for a financial remuneration, would use her connections on behalf of a likely young lady. Such arrangements were often made when a family had a daughter to marry off but lacked the social connections to match her well themselves. Lady Ruth Fitchett had been happy to take Emmie's money. Lady Ruth liked money and found ingenious ways of getting it and holding on to it.

The lady's maid was more difficult. An upper servant such as a lady's maid had to be presentable and somewhat educated. She attended to her mistress's intricate wardrobe, including its many layers and frills and, in the case of evening gowns, thousands of beads sewn onto fabric. She also arranged hair, accompanied her mistress on calls, when she shopped, and on country house visits, as well as attending to a thousand other personal details.

No lady of quality did without a personal maid. Emmie had counted on Dolly to play the part, but Dolly was involved in schemes of her own. Just in time Emmie remembered another friend, Betsy Nipper, who could do the job. Betsy was Turnip's niece, and her mother had been a lady's maid before she had been brought low by drink.

Meanwhile Emmie scrounged around her

rooms and found her old French and Latin dictionaries. She translated the foreign phrases in the packet of clues and struggled to divine their meaning. So far she'd been unsuccessful. Perhaps they would make sense once she got to Agincourt Hall.

Between the night of the North ball and the day she left for the country, Emmie saw the marquess several times at Society functions. Before an art exhibition, a musical evening given by Adelaide's mother, or a concert or opera, she would convince herself that she'd vanquished the fluttery confusion that threatened whenever she looked at Valin North. But although he sought her out and she never allowed him to see her alone, she fluttered anyway. Even more humiliating was the knowledge that she didn't trust *herself* when alone with the marquess, much less him. These skirmishes with herself made time pass tortuously.

Finally, on the appointed day, Emmie and Betsy Nipper drove through the grounds of the North family seat with Turnip on the coach box. Also with her was the street urchin, one of her gang, who would play her page. Emmie was proud of herself for thinking of the page. Having such an extra servant would proclaim her wealth to everyone and assure Valin North that she had no need of marrying for money. Thus he wouldn't have cause to suspect her of angling for his hand. Pilfer Oxleek was enterprising and bright enough to do the job, and he wouldn't cause comment among the other servants, since his position was as lowly as his station in life.

Pilfer sat beside Betsy, opposite Emmie, and craned his neck out the window as they drove down the avenue toward Agincourt Hall. "Coo! Look at all them trees, missus."

"Pilfer, I told you to say miss."

The boy nodded. "Yes, miss."

Emmie tried not to smile. Pilfer was small for his seven years and spoke in an oddly deep voice with a lisp and an air of gravity that startled most people. He would stand as tall as he could, look up at an adult with a frown, and say disconcerting things in a bass voice, such as, "What's the matter? Don't yer like children?"

"Ooo!" cried Betsy. "Emmie, I mean miss, look at that gatehouse. That there is a fortress, is that."

"Betsy, sit down. Lady's maids don't hang out the window and gawp at things."

"Sorry. I forgot. How old d'you think this place is?"

Emmie gazed at the high stone walls of the fortified manor. "The oldest parts are medieval, but most of it was built under the Tudors over three hundred years ago. I suppose it's been modified again and again."

"Cor," Betsy said in tones of wonder.

The carriage passed under the gatehouse and into a court that would have held half a dozen St. Giles boardinghouses. Turnip slowed the vehicle to a stately walk as they passed between two identical reflection pools.

"I read about this," Emmie said in hushed awe. "It's the Fountain Court."

As she spoke water shot into the air from dozens of spouts along the edge of the pools and from enormous tiered fountains set in their centers. The sound was entrancing; the sun pierced sprays of water, causing misty rainbows. Emmie was staring at the arcs of transparent color, or she would have seen the tall figure coming around the edge of one of the pools to meet the carriage. Instead she only glimpsed Valin North when Turnip stopped the vehicle. She turned to Betsy and Pilfer.

"It's him! Behave yourselves."

And you control yourself, Emmie thought as her stomach lurched at this unexpected encounter. She could see the gold-brown gleam of his hair through the fountain mist. *Stop that, Emmie Fox! Think about the treasure, not the man.* Glancing at her companions to see if they'd noticed her harried state, she composed her features and watched the marquess near the carriage.

Elegant, easy, and confident, Valin North opened the carriage door and inclined his head. "Ah, it's Miss de Winter. Welcome to Agincourt

Hall. Allow me to help you down. If you're not too fatigued from your journey, I'd be honored to show you some of my house."

Without waiting for her answer he held out his hand. To refuse would appear rude, something a lady never wished to do, especially in front of servants. She put her hand in his and got out of the carriage, no easy task in her voluminous traveling dress and crinoline. She was relieved to reach the ground without tipping the hoop over her head.

North spoke to Turnip. "Drive around the house. Thistlethwayte is the butler, and Mrs. Parker is the housekeeper. They will show you everything."

Turning to Emmie, he offered his arm and they walked slowly behind the carriage, until it vanished through a gate in the courtyard wall.

Gesturing to the pools and water sprays, North said, "This is the Fountain Court. Mostly for show, really, but I like to come when the sun is at the right angle to see the rainbows."

Emmie had been staring. Either the sound of the water or the magic of the rainbows was causing a thrill to run through her body. The cause couldn't be the feel of his arm beneath the layers of his clothing. She wouldn't allow it to be.

"I've never seen anything like it," she said.

He looked at her oddly, then smiled. "You're

kind, Miss de Winter, but you must have seen many like this in France."

A mistake already. She had to concentrate or she'd trip herself up.

"Still, this is very fine."

They continued into the next court with Emmie castigating herself and trying to be as alert and wary as she usually was when engaged in one of her schemes.

North described the Lion Court. "It's named for the statues of the North lions." He pointed to the animals perched at either end beside the gateways.

Emmie murmured her approval while she looked for anything that resembled the clues to the Spanish gold. According to the room assignments given by Beaufort, "Monsieur d'Or" was lodged in *"la chambre sur la spirale."* The chamber under the spiral. She wanted to find a spiral of some kind. Until she could make sense of the other foreign phrases, it was her only guide.

"I haven't seen Miss Cowper of late."

Startled out of her search, Emmie said, "What?"

"I said I haven't seen Miss Cowper lately." North had stopped beside a lion statue and was looking down at her.

"She's—she's gone home."

"So early in the Season? I thought I was the only one who left London in May."

"Miss Cowper found that her strength wasn't equal to remaining in town any longer."

"I hope she's not ill."

"No, only fatigued. She is already better now she's home."

Walking through the next gate, North said, "Now you'll see why I prefer Agincourt Hall to London."

Another step brought them into a courtyard framed by open-air galleries, each a series of rounded arches supported by columns covered in ivy. The house itself formed the fourth side of the court, a soaring structure in creamy stone with a shining leaded roof of fish-scale tiles. Emmie glimpsed rows of dormer windows, rounded turrets, and elegantly carved pilasters.

"How lovely." She made the mistake of looking at him, at those deep-set silver eyes, and said the first thing that occurred to her. "I've never seen anything like it."

He was looking at her oddly again. She'd said something wrong—again.

"You've never seen the chateaux of France?" he asked. "Just where was this French boarding school you attended, Miss de Winter?"

"Oh. Well—for shame, my lord. I try to compliment your house, and you find fault with me."

Emmie didn't breathe while she waited for him to respond. Drat this man. He made her feel as if there were mad butterflies in her brain. He was frowning at her, not in his usual ill-humored manner, but in confusion. Finally he smiled and bowed.

"You're right. Please forgive me." His arm swept around. "The garden is Italian, and too formal for my taste, but I love the galleries."

Relieved to have escaped another blunder, Emily glanced around the court. Then she turned to stare at the house again, aghast. She'd been looking for a spiral, and she'd found it, or rather, them. There were spirals everywhere. Spirals formed one of the elements of the friezes that separated the first and second floors, and the second and third floors. A pattern of sculptured wreaths, tendrils, grotesque figures, and spirals repeated itself over and over. Spirals decorated the architrave over the portal for the front door. They were on decorated piers that surmounted the architrave; they were on ornate gables carved over the dormer windows of the house. She even saw spirals on keystones in the rounded arches of the galleries.

"La chambre sur la spirale," Emmie muttered to herself.

"I beg your pardon?"

"Oh, nothing, my lord."

"You said something about a room. Are you tired?"

"No, no. I'm quite interested in architecture, although I don't know as much as I would wish."

"Allow me to give you a tour of the whole house, then."

"I should enjoy that," Emmie said. What luck. He was going to show her everything right away, and she'd get a better idea of where to start looking.

North offered his arm again. As Emmie laid her hand on his sleeve, he said, "Have you no quotations about houses with which to regale me?"

"I can think of none. Where are we going?"

"To the gallery," North said as he led her beneath a rounded arch and into darkness.

Emmie stopped at once. "I can't see."

"Wait a moment."

"I still can't see."

She felt his hands on her arms as she was turned away from the sunlight. "Don't look at the light or your eyes will never adjust."

Blinking rapidly Emmie found she could distinguish him standing in front of her. She could smell a hint of some clean-scented soap, and her mouth went dry. She cleared her throat and looked away from him. "What did you want to show me?"

"Do you really enjoy Shakespeare, Miss de Winter?"

"Yes, but what has that to do with—"

"Because since we've met I've been thinking."

"Yes?"

"I've never met a young lady who could quote Shakespeare, or who even wished to read him. You're different."

The sound of his voice zinged from her ears to her spine! She had to get away from him and compose herself. Drat. What was wrong with her that she couldn't play a part she'd managed easily in the past?

"I think we should go inside. I'm sure Lady Ottoline expects me."

"No, she doesn't. Listen to me, Emmie: 'Is it thy will thy image should keep open/ My heavy eyelids to the weary night?/ Dost thou desire my slumbers should be broken,/ While shadows like to thee do mock my sight?' "

She had always loved words, reading, and literature—what little she got of it—and now Valin's phrases lifted her into a world inhabited by them alone. If there was magic, it was in such words and images.

Valin touched her cheek, and Emmie started. Whirling around, crinoline tilting precariously, she rushed into the sunlight. She took refuge behind one of the lion statues. She was a lady. If she didn't remember that, she'd lose more than her chance to find the Spanish gold.

Valin had followed her. "Still my lady coward, I see."

"I'm more fatigued from my journey than I thought, my lord. Please show me into the house."

Grasping the lion's neck, he swung around the statue and grinned at her. "What makes you so different, Miss de Winter?"

"I'm sure I don't understand you."

Valin's smile vanished as he rounded the statue. He clasped his hands behind his back and stared at her in a musing manner. "You may fool everyone else, but not me."

"I fail to . . ." Had he discovered something? Emmie went cold.

"You have mysteries about you, Miss Emily de Winter, and I'm going to solve them."

"What fancies, my lord." Emmie lifted her skirts and walked up the stairs that led to the front door of Agincourt Hall.

North mounted the stairs two at a time and planted himself in front of her. "You're unnerved. I can see a tiny vein throbbing at your temple, and you're breathing as hard as if you'd ridden in the Derby." He narrowed his eyes as he regarded her. "I'm onto something, by Jove. And it's important, by the look of you. Who would have thought?" She tried to go around him, but he stepped in her way, bent over her, and smiled lazily. "What are you hiding, Miss Emily de Winter?"

Emmie gaped at him. To be nearly unmasked in so sudden a manner robbed her of speech. She might have stood there, her mouth hanging open like a dead fish, but the doors burst open behind North and disgorged his aunt.

"Dear Miss de Winter, how good of you to accept my invitation. Valin! Don't keep the dear girl standing in the hot sun. Come in, come in."

6

Valin was in the Russian room because no one ever came there. He was feeling guilty. Having allowed Aunt Ottoline to arrange this country house party, he had intended to approach it with the proper marriage-market attitude. With all sincerity, he'd expected to spend most of his time with the young ladies she invited. But it quickly became obvious that he would never be as important to Miss Kingsley as she was to herself. Lady Victoria was so in love with her Thoroughbreds he could hardly get her attention, and Lady Drusilla had the intelligence of a whelk. None of them would do; Aunt would be furious.

Valin settled in an armchair and tried to read *The Times*, but he was still bothered. It was because of Miss de Winter. She'd been at Agincourt Hall for almost two weeks, and he was spending too much time with her. The other guests were beginning to talk. The young ladies were annoyed and offended, but Valin didn't care. If any of them had been tolerable, he wouldn't have found Miss de Winter's company preferable. It wasn't his fault.

On top of this, he still hadn't returned her fan. He had a curious reluctance to part with it and give up the honeysuckle fragrance it bore. To make matters worse, he was feeling guilty for having done something unforgivable. Before she arrived he was already intrigued by Miss de Winter, and the day she arrived his curiosity had been piqued even more. After a week in her company, however, Emily de Winter had become a genuine mystery. So much of one that he'd hired a private inquiry agent to investigate her.

He had an evil mind; he'd become suspicious simply because the poor girl had tried to be nice to him by admiring his house and grounds. Oh, and because she didn't seem to know the relative rank of his various guests. Surely he could attribute such ignorance to her foreign upbringing. He would have if another suspicious question hadn't returned to annoy him. He still wasn't satisfied about her lack of even a trace of an accent. After having spent so many years in France Miss de Winter should have at least had difficulty with her *R*s.

"You bastard," he muttered. "She probably

spent months trying to Anglicize her speech to fit in."

No. He wasn't being unreasonable. There had been other incidents.

After dinner one night, he'd shown everyone the conservatory. While the others were admiring the tropical plants, he had found Miss de Winter inspecting the walls of the house that adjoined the glass structure. She'd been startled to see him appear from behind an ancient oak tree.

"What are you doing, Miss de Winter?" he'd asked.

Whirling around she sucked in her breath and stared at him for a moment. "Oh, just admiring the way the conservatory is constructed."

"You could see it better if you weren't right next to the wall."

"True." She hurried past him into the garden, and gazed up at the glass panels.

He joined her. "We had Bertie here last year, and he loved it."

"Who?"

Valin glanced down at Miss de Winter with a frown. "Even a girl from a French boarding school ought to know there's only one Bertie in England."

"Why?"

"Because he's the Prince of Wales."

"Oh, that Bertie," she said. "Shall we go in? The others will wonder where you are."

Valin shifted in his armchair and let *The Times* fall to his lap. He could have sworn she hadn't the least idea that Prince Albert Edward was known as Bertie. And there had been other small instances that made him suspicious of the elegant Miss de Winter.

She hadn't understood him when he referred to his cattle. Everyone he knew would have known he was referring to his horses, not real cattle. Miss de Winter had not. Then there was the way she'd complained about the bell that was rung at six o'clock in the morning. The other young ladies had blushed when Miss de Winter talked of it at breakfast. Why hadn't she known the bell was rung so that those married ladies and gentlemen who'd spent the night with their lovers could return to their proper rooms before the servants were up and about? Every schoolgirl knew that, even if they didn't understand what went on during those nighttime sojourns.

A few days ago he'd mentioned in passing that a distant relative "had his strawberry leaves." Her confusion told him she had no idea that he was referring to part of the design of a ducal coronet as a way of indicating that the man had succeeded to the title. That was when he decided to find out all he could about Miss Emily Charlotte de Winter, but now he was having regrets. Miss de Winter couldn't help having been raised in France. Her parents had done her a disservice leaving her there for so long. The poor girl was a stranger among her own kind, and he was about to find out how ridiculous were his suspicions.

He should have realized he was succumbing to his own habit of distrust. He expected people to disappoint, and if they didn't he found a way to make them. It was something he'd learned after his father had married his stepmother, Lady Carolina.

Valin closed his eyes and forced himself not to allow ugly memories into his mind. There wasn't time to think of Carolina, no time to torture himself with more guilt. The inquiry agent had arrived, and Thistlethwayte was showing him upstairs. Valin would listen to his no doubt harmless report, pay the man, and forget his own folly.

Valin's shoulders twitched in discomfort. He suspected himself of ignoble motives where Miss de Winter was concerned. He couldn't get her out of his thoughts. He heard her voice, low and provocative, when he was reading correspondence. He smelled her when he was out riding alone— that captivating scent of honeysuckle and Emily that always seemed to envelop him when he was with her. He saw her in the face of every woman he met, or, rather, he found himself wanting to see only her. He was a sick man.

Disgusted with himself, Valin jumped up from the chair in which he'd been sitting and went to one of the glass display tables arranged around the room. His grandfather had brought back dozens of expensive curiosities from his travels in Russia. He paused beside a pedestal on which rested a sixteenth-century gold chalice decorated in a niello pattern of floral scrolls. It was mounted with rubies, emeralds, and sapphires; his fingers traced the rim. The antique gold reminded him of the highlights in Emily's hair.

"Stop it. She's been here less than three weeks, and you're behaving like a madman."

He wandered over to look at the *kovsh,* a sixteenth-century Russian dipper, in one of the cases. Silver, with a high, elongated handle, it was shaped like a wide boat and was engraved with lions and griffins. The rim was lined with pearls. He focused on the toasting bowl next to the dipper. He'd always liked it because it had a pointed lid and was decorated with a raised foliate pattern. It had an inscription that his grandfather had said translated, "True love is like this golden vessel. It never breaks, and if it bends, it can be mended."

"Love," Valin whispered. "First you have to be worth loving before your love can bend or mend."

A knock sent him hastening for his chair. He sat

and picked up *The Times* as Thistlethwayte entered followed by a stranger.

"Mr. Mildmay, my lord."

Valin had hired Ronald Mildmay upon the recommendation of a friend and hadn't met the man before. He was surprised and impressed that Mildmay was dressed like a gentleman in a well-cut coat, silk tie, and boots obviously made in Bond Street. The inquiry agent had a dour, regretful manner, as if he were a long-suffering parent to the continually misbehaving world. He was slight, with sloping shoulders, thinning dark hair, and a nose shaped like the Russian dipper in the display case.

Mildmay began immediately after the introductions were over. "Your lordship realizes that I needed more time. My report is extremely preliminary."

"Get on with it, man. You found nothing, did you? Well, I expected as much. A foolish whim on my part—"

"Oh, no, my lord. I found something, or rather, it's what I didn't find that's suspicious."

Valin went cold. He dropped the newspaper and rose. "Let's have it. What did you find?"

Mildmay opened a document case he had been carrying and referred to the papers within it. "From what my inquiries have uncovered, my lord, there is no such person as Miss Emily Charlotte de Winter."

"The de Winters are in DeBrett's. My copy is old, so I assumed—"

"No branch of the family has a daughter named Emily Charlotte, or even a lady of the right age," Mildmay said sorrowfully. He sighed. "As you instructed, my agents were careful not to reveal their purpose when inquiring at the houses of the families with whom she's stayed. However, we are certain that no one ever met Miss de Winter before a few weeks ago. Her only connection with society is the Honorable Miss Agnes Cowper, whom we cannot find, either."

"I told you, she's in Northumberland."

"She's not where we can find her, my lord. And an elderly lady like that shouldn't be so hard to discover."

Mildmay closed his document case. "The details would bore you, my lord, but I may summarize by saying that I could find no tradesmen who could attest to Miss de Winter's presence in London for more than those few weeks I mentioned. A respectable person of her position would have dealt with at least some of them—purveyors of fine lace, corsets, the more expensive fabrics and headgear. No blacksmith, livery, or domestic service agency has had anything to do with her."

"And that means?" Valin asked.

Mildmay glanced around at the Russian gold. "It means, my lord, that it's likely that the lady in question is an imposter, a refined adventuress out to steal from you, or—"

"Or what?" Valin snapped.

"Or she has grander designs." Mildmay shook his head in grief. "Designs upon your lordship's heart and hand."

Valin turned away from the agent, staring at the gold chalice but not seeing it. "My heart and hand?" he said faintly.

"Forgive me, but as she's been here so long, that appears to be likely." Mildmay placed the documents on one of the display cases. "A simple robbery would require only a short stay during which she could locate the desired objects. She would then leave and send minions to do the actual robbery."

"So, that's how it's done," Valin said without interest.

"Often, my lord, but in this case—"

"Thank you, Mildmay. Thistlethwayte has a cheque for you. Should I need anything else, I shall call upon you."

Mildmay was a man of discretion who knew when to make himself invisible, and this he did.

Valin heard the door close and walked blindly to the window. It looked out over the eighteenth-century terraced gardens at the back of the house.

He'd been suspicious, and yet to be faced with the truth was a shock. She was an imposter. Perhaps she'd been born into a good family that had fallen upon hard times. Certainly Emily, or whatever her name was, had been educated and trained as a lady. Certainly she was clever, more than clever. She was brilliant. Valin glared at the documents Mildmay had left behind. She had him panting after her like a puppy, curse her soul.

Was she after his heart and hand? Was she like all the rest, interested in his title and riches? Dear God, she was ruthless. She'd twisted his guts around her ivory fan.

Valin swore, whipped around, and started pacing. "Bloody liar! Vicious, deceitful creature. I'll toss her out on her ear, I will. Dear God, if only it were permissible to raise one's hand to a woman."

"Va—lin!"

He winced at the mad-parrot screech. The door flew open, and Aunt Ottoline soared in on a wave of apricot silk with yellow bows.

Valin squinted at the garish effect, sunk his hands in his pockets, and grumbled, "Yes, Aunt. I'm extremely busy at the moment. I'm due to meet Miss de Winter. We're going for a drive around the park."

"Not until I have a word with you."

"Only one?"

"Don't be impudent, Valin. I boxed your ears when you were a boy, and I can do it again."

Breathless and pink with agitation, Ottoline subsided into a chair, battered her enormous skirts into submission, and turned her glittering stare on Valin.

"It was you who came to me, Valin. Months ago you threw yourself on my mercy, and begged me to help you find a suitable girl to marry in order to save Agincourt Hall from Acton's depredations. Then you behave as if I am persecuting you when I do my best to help you."

"I'm sorry, Aunt."

"I declare I shall fall into a brain fever if you don't mend your conduct."

In his preoccupation, he barely heard her. "I will, Aunt."

"Good." Ottoline patted her lace cap and folded her hands in her lap. "Now, who is it to be: Miss Kingsley, Lady Drusilla, or Lady Victoria?"

"I don't care for any of them," Valin said absently. Then he started at the high, gooselike wail that echoed off the walls.

"Va—lin!"

Ottoline fell back in her chair, sputtering and moaning. Alarmed at her color, Valin rushed to her, found her scent bottle, and held it under her nose.

"Aunt, don't carry on so. I can't help it. None of those girls is congenial to me."

"No one ever will be!" Ottoline sniffed and tossed her head from side to side. She was flushed and breathing rapidly. "I'm undone. No one knows what I suffer. Oh, my heart, it flutters so, and my head is pounding. Oh, oh!"

When his aunt's face turned crimson, Valin grabbed his newspaper and fanned her with it. "Shall I call a doctor? Truly, Aunt, you don't look well."

"I shall be disgraced. Everyone in Society knows I'm arranging your marriage. The families of the girls you've rejected will hate me, and everyone else will laugh at me."

Ottoline began searching for her handkerchief. Valin found it for her, and she covered her nose with it.

"I know what you think of me, Nephew. You think me a ridiculous old woman, and perhaps I am. But I love you, and I've tried to help you."

It was Valin's turn to redden. All this time he'd thought only of his own difficulties while making his aunt suffer for her good-hearted attempts to help him.

"I'm a swine, Aunt. Can you forgive me?"

Ottoline's face had gone pale. "Nephew, I really cannot go on with this misery." She touched his hand and he felt how cold hers was. "You like none of the girls I invited?"

Shaking his head, Valin felt a stab of guilt when his aunt's eyes filled with tears. He felt even worse when she began to sob. This wasn't the theatrical crying of a spoiled woman, but the sincere weeping of a lady who felt defeat.

"Don't cry, Aunt." Dear God, he was a monster. "I promise, I'll choose from among the next group to whom you introduce me."

This only brought a wail and renewed weeping. At a loss, Valin searched for the scent bottle. It had fallen on the carpet, and as he picked it up, Valin's glance fell upon the papers that incriminated Emily de Winter. An idea leaped into his head, and Valin didn't pause to examine its consequences. He would pretend to become engaged. Then Aunt would be satisfied, and he could search for a bride without interference, without Society's glaring attention. He'd been unwise to do anything else.

"Please, Aunt, don't upset yourself. I—I was going to wait until I'd settled everything, but since you're so distressed, I'll tell you now. I'm going to marry Emily de Winter."

Ottoline's sniffles ceased abruptly. She blinked wetly at him. "Miss de Winter? Are you mad? She's almost foreign, and we barely know her."

"I barely know any of the girls you've thrown at—asked me to consider."

"But, Valin, there are so many other more suitable young ladies."

"Now, Aunt, you were just in a terrible state because I wouldn't decide. Well, I have decided, and that's that."

Ottoline sat up and sniffed. "I don't believe you."

"What? Why not?"

"Emily is presentable, but not nearly the beauty your rank requires in a wife, and she has none of the connections that would recommend her to the family. Why would your eye fall on her?"

"Why?" Valin's mind went blank for a moment. He hadn't expected her to disbelieve him. "Why—er . . . Because we're in love, deeply and passionately in love."

Ottoline frowned at him. "You haven't acted like you're in love."

"Been hiding it."

"Why?"

"Wanted to be sure first."

His aunt leaned toward him and placed her hand on his arm. "Are you certain, Nephew? I shouldn't want you to make a bad marriage out of a whim."

"I'm sure," Valin said. "I'm in love, like Romeo, Othello, King Arthur."

"Valin, those people all died, and anyway, they're not real."

"I know what I'm doing. Depend upon it."

"The rest of the family will not approve."

"I don't care."

Fanning her face with her handkerchief, Ottoline rose. "I know you don't, Valin. But if you've chosen the wrong girl, you'll soon care, very much indeed."

7

❦

Emmie plopped to the floor in the middle of her crinoline and petticoats, blew a stray tendril of hair off her nose, and groaned.

"What am I going to do, Betsy?"

Betsy was standing on a chair holding a traveling skirt in her outstretched arms. "About what, 'is lordship?"

"No, not him! What makes you say him? Why should I be worried about him? I'm not worried about him. I'm worried about finding the gold."

"I looked everywhere below-stairs," Betsy said. "There ain't no spirals in the servants' areas. Come on, now. You got to hook it if you're going to be ready for that carriage drive with yer follower."

Emmie popped up and glared at her friend. "He's not my follower. I told you, he has a reputation for seducing women, and I think he pays attention to me out of habit." Tossing her head, Emmie continued. "I'm not the one making a spectacle of myself over him. All the unmarried girls and half the married ladies here want him. The marquess sets their hearts fluttering just by walking into a room."

"Wot's all this about fluttering?"

"It's how he moves," Emmie said between gritted teeth. "He does it on purpose." When Betsy lifted her brows, Emmie stamped her foot. "Oh, I don't know. It's—it's the kind of walk I'd expect from a wolf stalking in a dark forest."

"Oh, I know what kind he is all right. You look sharp, Emmie, or he'll do for you. That one will have you in his bed before you know it."

Emmie didn't reply. She was having a difficult time maintaining her adversarial attitude toward "'is lordship," especially since hearing so much about him from the servants' gossip Betsy imparted. It was cursed hard to summon up contempt for a man who seemed to spend most of his time fighting for the welfare of wounded veterans, widows, and their children. Why couldn't he have been selfish and stupid? Then playing her role would have been so easy. She had to preserve an attitude of detachment. Everything depended upon it.

"Wake up and stir yourself, my girl," Betsy said.

Emmie held up her arms, and Betsy dropped the skirt over her head. She fought her way into it, then slipped into the bodice. Betsy turned her around and began fastening the buttons in the back, and muttering at the same time.

"What are you grumbling about now?" Emmie asked, still wallowing in her ill humor.

"This here dress. I never see'd no ladies in wine-colored traveling dresses. Black is what's respectable."

"The whole idea was to get myself noticed and attract the interest of the marquess."

"Well, you done that, all right."

Throwing up her hands, Emmie rounded on her friend. "How was I supposed to know he'd be so difficult to handle. All the other men I've dealt with have been manageable. They've been gentlemen."

"Yes, but this one's not just a gentleman, he's a lord and used to getting what he wants."

"I'll manage him."

"So far it looks like he's managing you," Betsy said as she fought Emmie's unruly curls to mastery with hairpins.

"I don't know what you're talking about."

"He's got you dithering and distracted, he has. Who was it who came back to her room all flustered last night saying as how the marquess had got her alone after dinner and tried to kiss her?"

Emmie avoided Betsy's amused gaze and sat down at the vanity so that her friend could put a bonnet on her head. She stared into the mirror, then scowled at her reflection when she realized her face was crimson. North had indeed got her alone after dinner, but Emmie could have escaped him had she tried hard. Instead, a strange compulsion had kept her there as surely as if the marquess were a sorcerer who drew her to him with some black magic incantation. Was this how he seduced all those other women she'd heard about? How dare this foul-tempered aristocrat turn her into a goggle-eyed slave? To cover her bewilderment Emmie burst into speech.

"He's a sneaking varmint. I left the ladies after dinner to fetch a shawl, and he was waiting for me by the stairs." She pounded the vanity. "He doesn't care about me. He's just amusing himself because he's bored with the other women his aunt invited. I'd like to throttle him."

When Betsy sniggered, Emmie turned slowly and asked, "What are you giggling at?"

"You like his attentions."

"I beg your pardon?" Emmie said as she drew herself up.

"If Dolly was here she'd give you the truth of it, too." Betsy finished tying the bonnet and rested her hands on her hips. "I ain't never seen you all bothered and alarmed over any man."

"Exactly."

"Until now."

"I'm not bothered!"

"Oh, the devil," Betsy said with a grin. "Your heart is fluttering worse than any o' them fine ladies', only you know how to hide it, being from the streets and all. But he's in your blood, Emmie. It's all you can do to keep from staring at him whenever he's about."

Fumbling with the bow at her chin, Emmie sniffed. "You're imagining things. I'm simply annoyed because his attentions have interfered with my ability to search for the gold."

"Oh, I don't blame you, mind. He's a right handsome devil. I think it's the way he don't seem to be trying to woo the ladies that makes 'em want him all the more. There he is, his pretty face all screwed up in a fearful scowl what makes you realize how much power and passion is locked up inside him."

"Betsy," Emmie said as she rose to leave, "you're depraved."

Ignoring Betsy's guffaw, Emmie marched out of the house to find a light gig waiting for her. Its top was down and a groom held the pair of horses that drew it. She had understood that Lady Fitchett and Miss Kingsley were to make up the party, but the others weren't here, and the gig would hold only two people. There weren't going to be any drives alone with Valin North. She was halfway up the steps when North charged out of the house, caught her firmly by the arm, and hurried her toward the gig.

"Good afternoon, Miss de Winter."

"I cannot drive without Lady Fitchett. Perhaps tomorrow—"

Without slowing down, North said, "Lady Fitchett has a slight headache, but she said to go without her."

The groom steadied the matched pair of grays as they reached the gig. In spite of Emmie's protests, North propelled her into the vehicle and took his place beside her.

"Really, my lord, I must insist that we wait."

Emmie gathered her skirts and tried to get up, but North slapped the reins. The gig jumped into motion and Emmie was thrown back into the seat.

"Stop this carriage at once."

"Not now," North said without looking at her.

"If you don't, I'll jump," Emmie said.

"I wouldn't. You'll break your neck at this speed."

The gig bounced over a rut, and Emmie clutched at the door for balance with one hand and held her bonnet on with the other. They careened down the drive, turned onto one of the paths that crossed the park, and plunged into a wood. Holding on to the gig so that she wasn't bounced against North, Emmie darted glances at her abductor.

His harsh profile registered more than his usual annoyance. Something had happened to make him furious. His eyes reminded her of cold polished marble and his movements were quick and sharp, as though he were containing a violence he dared not release.

Suddenly North swung the gig off the path and walked the horses through the trees until they came to a stream that twisted and danced through the wood. Tying the reins, he turned and subjected her to a disgusted examination as though she were a piglet that had taken a bath in dung. No doubt his aunt had been hectoring him about his choice of a suitable wife. Whatever had made him angry, he had no right to take it out on her.

"This is most improper, my lord. I insist you take me back at once."

North allowed his gaze to slice down her figure, linger on her bosom and hips, then rise to her face again. Such behavior would have flustered most women. Emmie had punched drunken navvies for lesser insults. She lifted a brow and stared back at him.

"By God, you're a bold piece!"

Emmie's brows met in the middle of her forehead. "Don't shout at me."

"Pestilence and death!"

He grabbed her by the arms. Pulling her close, he held her so that their noses almost touched and shouted, "Who are you!"

Emmie had been fighting him, but at this question she went still. She retreated to the cold, calm place in her mind. It was where she always went when in danger. The cold place enabled her to smooth her features into a mask of slightly amused derision.

"There will be no further conversation until you release me."

Blinking in surprise, North let her go. Her tone seemed to have brought him out of his rage for the moment, for he spoke instead of shouted.

"Who are you?" He shook his head as her mouth opened to form a denial. "Don't waste my time. I set an inquiry agent the task of finding out all he could about you. He's of the opinion that the Honorable Miss Emily de Winter doesn't exist." North leaned toward her, causing Emmie to put her back against the carriage door. "If you don't like me touching you, tell me the truth."

Emmie remained silent and evaluated her chances of making him believe another lie. They weren't great. And if she angered him, he might lose control of that volcanic temper. She was about to speak, but North was ahead of her.

"Don't bother to lie. I already know part of it.

You're a lady adventuress out to trap a wealthy husband."

Luckily for Emmie, her mouth already open. She stared at him for a moment, then popped it shut.

"I've already realized that you must have had some sort of genteel upbringing. You've comported yourself excellently, considering your background. Was your father a clerk, or was he a solicitor?" North paused, but his impatience drove him on. "Well? Don't goggle at me like a scandalized parlor maid. Answer me."

"Oh, gracious mercy." She was thinking fast.

"It remains to be seen whether you'll get mercy or not. Now speak up, woman."

"Very well." Emmie relaxed, smoothed her rumpled skirts, and gave a rueful sigh, her eyes downcast. "You're right, of course. I should have known I wouldn't be able to deceive someone as clever as you, my lord."

"I can do without the shy maiden performance, and the flattery, too."

She shot an angry look at him but dropped her humble attitude.

"You wanted the truth, my lord, and you're going to get it. My parents are dead. My father was a doctor with a successful practice in Shrewsbury, but he had squandered his fortune and my inheritance on liquor, cards, and horse racing by the

time I was twelve. I have nothing, but I was raised
to be a lady. Penniless ladies have no recourse for
earning a living except being a governess or a
companion to some wealthy elderly lady. Either
means a life of undependable servitude and certain
loneliness. In desperation I sought another avenue
by which to escape destitution."

"By lying and trying to trap me into marriage."

Emmie flushed. "You self-righteous prig. Have
you ever been poor? No. Ever gone for days without anything to eat? No. Slept in a doorway in the
freezing rain? No. Pray pardon me for not liking
such conditions, but some of us baseborn criminals
are odd that way."

She jerked herself around to face forward in the
gig. Her gloved fingers drummed on the door
frame, sounding loud in the silence that fell between them.

"I'm sorry."

Turning her head, Emmie eyed the marquess
with distrust. "I beg your pardon, my lord?"

"I said I was sorry. I know what it's like to be
cold and hungry and in fear for your life." At her
questioning look, he gave her a slight smile. "The
Crimea, you see."

"Oh."

His smile vanished. "However, you don't have
the right to invade my life and—blast. This isn't

what I wanted to talk about. I wanted to make a bargain with you."

Suspicious, Emmie asked, "What kind of bargain?"

"I want you to pose as my fiancée."

"You just said you didn't want to marry me," Emmie snapped.

"I don't, but I need someone to whom I can be engaged so that all the husband-hunting mamas and their daughters will leave me alone."

She hadn't expected her heart to hurt when he admitted he didn't want to marry her. She felt a stab, as though a shard of glass had pierced her chest. Drat and damnation, she couldn't reveal herself! What abject humiliation, and how foolish and absurd of her. She didn't want to marry this evil-tempered devil.

"I think not, my lord. You're quite capable of defending yourself against the onslaught of an army of mamas. I shall leave in the morning and cause you no further inconvenience."

"I won't allow you to leave."

"I shall leave."

To prove her point, Emmie turned the handle on the door of the gig and opened it. As she got up, North grasped her arm and hauled her back against him. Emmie reacted as she had hundreds of times before in the rookeries. She twisted snakelike and rammed her fist into North's stomach.

He released her with a gasp, and she jumped to
the ground. Lifting her skirts, Emmie sped toward
the path. She hadn't gone far before hands fastened
on her waist and she was lifted off her feet. She
landed over North's shoulder, her head dangling at
his back.

Emmie pounded on her captor's back. "Let go
of me, you bloody bastard!"

"What language, and from the daughter of a
respectable doctor."

"I'll throttle you, I will," Emmie shouted. "I'll
do you a mischief, see if I don't. I'll have you
scragged." She tried to kick him, but North had
hold of both her legs.

Arching her back, Emmie tried to writhe out of
his grasp, but North only slapped her on her bottom through the substantial padding of her petticoats and skirts. "Be still or I'll drop you, and
watch your language, or everyone will soon discover you've been frequenting places you
shouldn't have."

"Curse you for a sodding—ow!" He'd slapped
her on her bottom again. "You hit me, you
bloody—ow!"

Emmie felt herself being tossed in the air. She
landed in North's arms, her bonnet askew. Red
from being jounced and held upside down, she
glared up at her tormentor only to find him grinning at her. Before she could swear at him again,

he deposited her into the gig. She scrambled to the other door, but her skirt caught. Emmie turned to free it and found North had grabbed a handful of the fabric. She tried to yank it free, but he resisted without effort, smirking all the while.

"Let go o' me, you blood—" She thought better of her choice of words. "You sneaking devil."

"When you're playing my fiancée you'll have to remember not to get upset. When you're upset, your language suffers, and I detect a hint of the gutter."

"Oooo!"

Emmie kicked him. North yelped, but lunged at her before she could get away, landing on top of her. Emmie began to twist and writhe again, but her struggle only tangled their arms and legs and then plunged her beneath him on the seat. He was heavy, and with the binding of her corset and her exertions it was hard to breathe.

"You sodding arse, get off me."

He wasn't listening. He was glaring at her and breathing hard as though still in pain. His eyes traced the lines of her mouth, then lowered to her breasts beneath the covering of her bodice. Somehow his face drew closer, until their mouths almost touched. Emmie felt paralyzed, alarmed, but at the same time, drawn.

His lips brushed hers gently, teasing, and then

he whispered. "So this is the way to keep you from using foul language."

Sucking in her breath, Emmie let out a scream of outrage.

North gasped, covered his ears, and scrambled away from her. "Not so loud."

Emmie pushed herself upright and backed as far away from him as she could. North settled against the squabs, folded his arms, and grinned at her.

"Are you ready to be sensible?"

Emmie nodded grudgingly.

"Excellent. Now, as I was saying. You will play the part of my loving fiancée for, say, three months. That should be enough time for me to find a suitable and bearable young woman to marry. I'll be able to search in peace, unmolested by mamas and free of my aunt's well-meaning but unfortunate efforts."

"What if you don't find this paragon in three months?"

North sighed. "Ah, then you'll just have to stay on until I do."

"No."

"Yes."

Emmie folded her arms and snorted. "You fool. I'll simply sneak away at night, and you'll never find me."

"I won't look," North replied with a dismissive glance. "I'll put a bounty on your head so high your own mother would turn you in to me. Or can you tell me all your friends are trustworthy?"

Emmie wanted to slap that mocking smile off his face.

"You're a regular cunning sneak, you are. I bet your father was proud of you."

North lowered his gaze for a brief moment, then looked up with a bitter smile. "No, he wasn't, but never mind about my father. You admit you have no choice."

"I admit nothing."

"We'll begin at once."

North reached for her, and Emmie knocked his hands aside. She cried out in protest when he pulled her toward him.

"Be still, you little beast. Your hair is a mess and your bonnet's down your back. I want you presentable when we return and announce our engagement to the family."

Emmie shoved him away. "Don't touch me."

Sitting back, North watched her as she tried to repair the damage done by their struggle. After a while, he spoke musingly.

"You've been keeping rough company."

She didn't answer.

"What's your real name?"

"Emily Charlotte de Winter. Miss de Winter to you."

North gave her a disbelieving look, but she didn't correct herself.

"Very well," he said. "I've at least three months to find out."

Emmie's hands stilled on her bonnet ribbons. "My name really is Emily."

"Emily what?"

"Just Emily."

"You have to have a last name," he said as he moved her hands aside and took the bonnet ribbons.

Emmie stared over his shoulder as he tied a bow beneath her chin. He was too near. She could feel him even through the insubstantial tether of those silk ribbons. She wanted to touch his cheek with her fingertips, which made her angry, because she also wanted to spit at him, so she just glared at a tree outside the carriage. If she looked into his eyes, she would get herself into terrible trouble. North finished the bow but didn't move away.

His breath brushed her cheek as he said quietly, "I think I'm looking forward to the next three months, Emily No-name. And you're furious because you don't want to admit you are, too."

8

Almost an hour after her confrontation with Valin North, Emmie galloped through Agincourt Park beside the stream that had witnessed her humiliation. She jumped her mare over the water and slowed to a trot as she entered a clearing in the wood. The sun was still bright, although it was beginning its descent in the west.

In the clearing a white Greek folly sat like a decayed pearl on a deserted beach, the fancy of some bygone North. Aunt Ottoline had mentioned that it was modeled on the *tholos,* a round building with a conical roof supported by an arcade of columns. Originally a rustic retreat for the family, it had been allowed to fall into disrepair. Ivy covered the Ionic columns. The steps leading up to the arcade were cracked, and the interior had become the home of owls and spiders.

Betsy, Turnip, and Pilfer were waiting for her when Emmie trotted up to the folly and dismounted. She hiked her skirts above her ankles and stomped up the steps without a word. The others followed.

Once inside, Emmie let out a bellow that bounced off the stone walls. Her companions jumped at the noise, and Pilfer goggled as she paced around in a circle cursing Valin North.

Betsy gawked at her, too. "Wot's wrong?"

"She's been took mad," Pilfer said with awe.

"Nah," replied Turnip. "It's that marquess. He's the only one can set her going like that."

Emmie rounded on them breathing hard. "May he burn in hell. May God forsake him and all his descendents. I hope he's cursed with boils and rashes and fevers and his hair falls out and his nose rots off."

"Coo!" Pilfer exclaimed.

Betsy grabbed Emmie by the arms. "Wot's he done now?"

Having spent some of her rage, Emmie recounted the disaster by the stream.

"And now I've got to pretend to be his fiancée. I'd rather eat raw sheep entrails. The vile, deceitful varmint, expecting me to pretend to be something I'm not."

Pilfer rocked back and forth on his heels. "But that's what you do, missus."

"It's different."

"How?" Pilfer asked in his deep child-voice.

"I don't claim to be a high and mighty lord, a gentleman of honor."

Pilfer only stared at her with a puzzled frown. Emmie sighed and ruffled his hair.

"Just take my word, Pilfer. Valin North is a foul toad." She turned to Betsy and Turnip. "Which is why we've got to find the gold and scarper. Sooner or later he's bound to find out I'm not even the lady adventuress he assumes I am. Then we're for it."

"But me and Turnip already searched everywhere," Betsy said.

Turnip counted on his fingers. "We bin inna servants' hall, the kitchen and pantry, the still-room, the game larder and scullery. Betsy done looked over the washhouse, and I bin inna fish, ice, and coal rooms. Poor Betsy near got herself caught sneaking inna butler's pantry and house-keeper's room. No spirals."

"Then you can search the towers that are shut up," Emmie replied. "It will be a chance for you to use your old lock-picking skills, Turnip. Check the Stable Tower, the Venetian Tower, and the Moon Tower."

Betsy rolled her eyes and groaned. "All them

winding stairs. They go from the cellars up past the roof, you know."

"I know," Emmie said. "And I'll search the rest of the house that's of the right age, and the Gallery Tower since it's still open. There're no guests staying in it at the moment, but you never know when someone might wander in. I can claim to be exploring for my own amusement." Emmie grimaced. "After all, it's my future home. And I'll keep studying the foreign phrases. They must relate to this house and the gold, somehow."

"So . . ." Betsy eyed Emmie. "We got to stay here 'til his lordship finds a replacement for you. Hmmm."

"Don't you go saying hmmm to me, Betsy Nipper. I know what you're thinking."

"Me?"

Betsy was all innocence. Pilfer sniggered and Turnip gave him a gentle cuff on the head.

"Now you three listen," Emmie said, wagging her finger at them. "When we find this gold, we'll be rich enough to buy ten lords like his high-and-mightiness. I'll not have you speculating about me and him. There is no me and him. There's only him, and me." She gave an exasperated sigh. "I mean there's him. And there's me. Oh, never mind!"

She sent Betsy, Turnip, and Pilfer away and

watched them whispering and glancing at her over their shoulders as they went.

It was all Emmie could do not to scream and startle the horse. Valin North had ruined all the kindly feelings she had toward him, the toad.

No. She ought to be glad. Now she could hate him for threatening her plan to win security for her family. And hate him she did. Emmie repeated such thoughts to herself all the way home, never once admitting aloud how his touch had excited her even as she burned with anger and fought him in that carriage by the stream.

By the time she had gotten back to Agincourt Hall and sought the refuge of her room, Emmie had convinced herself she felt—if not hatred—at least a fervent dislike.

Soon Betsy appeared to announce it was time to dress for dinner. Her friend was buttoning the last of dozens of pearl buttons at the back of Emmie's silk gown when a housemaid arrived with a note from the marquess summoning his fiancée to his study.

"What presumption," Emmie muttered as she waited for Betsy to finish weaving imitation pearls through her hair. She watched her friend in the mirror. "Thinks he can order me about. Make me do what he wants."

"Well," Betsy said, "he can."

"Not for long, Betsy my dear, and not without

a cost. And that's what I'm going to show him tonight."

Betsy looked at Emmie. "Bless my eyes. I know that expression you got on your face. What are you planning?"

Picking up a lace handkerchief, Emmie rose silently.

As Emmie left, Betsy called out, "Just you take care. If you make him really furious, he'll smash us all."

The maid was waiting outside her door and Emmie followed her to the marquess's study. As the young woman opened the door in response to North's summons, a long pointed nose darted through the gap. Emmie bent down, made a fist, and slowly offered it to the collie that stood in her way.

"Hello, there," she said gently. Her hand was sniffed. The dog's tail began to swish back and forth, and Emmie patted the creature on the chest. "Good girl. You're a sweetie, yes, you are. You're such a pretty girl."

"Are you going to talk to my dog the whole evening or come inside?"

Emmie straightened to find Valin North standing over her, his habitual frown causing him to look like an offended war god. Ignoring his irritation, Emmie sailed by him with the dog at her heels. She sat down in a leather wing-back chair without being asked, and her new friend settled beside her on the floor. Emmie draped her arm over the side of the chair and stroked the dog's head.

She used this interlude to collect herself, because seeing the marquess in so intimate a setting had aroused a strange excitement in her that had nothing to do with her anger. Without trying, he exuded some kind of male seductiveness that was almost occult in its strength. The dog touched her cold nose to the back of Emmie's hand, and Emmie smiled to cover her disquiet.

North scowled at the dog. "Megan, you're a traitor."

"Nonsense," Emmie said, shaking off the effects of his presence. "Dogs and cats can sense a person's true character."

"She likes me, too, you know."

"Then, as improbable as it may seem to me, you must have some tolerable qualities that remain hidden to the world."

"Tolerable, eh? Only tolerable."

"That's as charitable as I can be given your conduct, my lord."

"I wouldn't sit in judgement if I were you, my lady No-name."

"What do you want, my lord?"

North went to a side table and poured two glasses of sherry. Offering Emmie one, he said,

"We should come to an understanding before the announcement of our engagement."

"I thought we'd done that."

"I mean an understanding about your behavior."

Emmie lifted her chin. "My conduct is above reproach."

"Oh, you can play the lady well," North said with a slight smile, "but I'm talking about your behavior toward me. No one's going to believe we're engaged if you treat me like a—"

"Scoundrel? Arrogant, rude, foul-tempered beast?"

"I was going to say enemy."

Emmie stopped stroking Megan. "I'm afraid it's beyond even my powers to pretend to love a presumptuous, deceitful, overbearing tyrant."

She gasped when North swiftly set his glass down, planted his hands on the arms of her chair, and leaned over her. Dark and menacing, he growled at her.

"That's enough. You, my lady adventuress, are going to play the part of a loving, doting, besotted young bride-to-be, or I'll . . ."

Regaining her composure, Emmie lifted a brow. "Or you'll expose me and defeat your own purpose?"

North glared at her, but the glare changed to a nasty smile as he looked at her. "There are other means of retaliation. Ones I seem to recall had you quite flustered."

Emmie's head sank into the leather chair back as North moved closer. Her hands came up and pressed against the expensive cloth of his evening coat. Before she could shove him away, his lips were so close they almost touched hers.

"Are you going to be a good little fiancée, Emmie?"

Her throat was too dry. She couldn't make her lips move. She'd lost her voice. Emmie's nails dug into his coat as she stared into the gray depths of his eyes. She could feel his breath on her lips. *If she moved, what would happen?* Her senses seemed magnified, and to her alarm she almost closed the tiny distance between them. *Emmie Fox, don't you dare move.* She mustered all her will in the effort. Then his whisper sent chills down her arms.

"Say you'll be a good girl, Emmie, or I'll kiss you."

Swallowing hard, she managed to say, "All right! Now get away from me."

With a chuckle he straightened and perched on the edge of his desk. "I knew you'd see reason. We'll get along much better once you learn to be agreeable and sensible."

"Biddable and submissive?" she snapped.

"Indeed."

Emmie rose and gave North a brittle smile that

would have set Betsy to shaking her head. "I shall be the deliriously happy and triumphant debutante."

"Excellent. Shall we join the others in the drawing room?"

A nod was all she could manage without screeching at him. Emmie hid her fury and made a convincing entrance when they joined the party gathered in the gold-and-blue drawing room in the wing opposite North's study. Each of them circulated among their friends and acquaintances, and Emmie was able to stay away from the marquess until dinner. Unfortunately, she found she'd been seated on his right at the huge dining table, an arrangement that must have been ordered by Aunt Ottoline. After desert was served, Emmie listened as North called for silence and made the dreaded proclamation.

"And so, my friends, I have the honor to announce my engagement to Miss Emily Charlotte de Winter."

There was silence, then a burst of exclamations and applause. Across the table Lady Fitchett beamed at her, which told Emmie that North had already informed her of the match. No doubt the old lady would claim Emmie's good fortune was due to her influence and expect a bonus payment. An adversity for which she had the marquess to thank. Another was the animosity with which she was being regarded by Miss Kingsley, the other debutantes, and their mamas.

North was still on his feet. "A toast, ladies and gentlemen." He raised his wineglass and caught Emmie's eye with a slight smirk. "To my lovely and charming bride-to-be, Miss de Winter."

"To Miss de Winter!" the rest echoed.

Her cheeks burning, Emmie murmured her thanks and darted a look of fury at North. Then she remembered her resolution.

"Thank you, my lord." She turned to Aunt Ottoline with a brilliant smile. "I declare, your nephew has taken me quite by surprise." Emmie raised her voice a little. "Did you know that our affection has entirely banished his dour temperament? Gracious mercy, he smiles all the time now."

"Really?" Ottoline replied with skepticism.

Everyone looked at North, who was scowling at Emmie.

"He's not smiling now, my dear," said Ottoline. "Honestly, Valin, who would believe you've just announced your engagement if they beheld that sour face of yours?"

Emmie smiled sweetly at North as she watched him struggle to master his ire. Eventually, with everyone staring at him, he contrived a pained smile that brought exclamations of approval and delight from family and friends. Only Emmie took note of the way his hands balled into fists or the searing glances he threw at her when he thought himself unobserved.

Serves you right, Emmie thought. *It'll do you good to have to play a distasteful part along with me.*

Emmie watched North struggle to maintain an air of good humor. He would forget his new role as he sipped wine. His mouth would settle into its customary frown, but soon he'd remember with a start, glance around the table guiltily, and force himself to adopt a pleasant air.

Each time this happened he'd give Emmie a fulminating and resentful look, then he'd be forced to mold his features into a more agreeable facade. It was all Emmie could do not to burst into a chortle. She was saved from disgracing herself when Ottoline led the ladies out of the dining room.

They settled in the salon where Miss Kingsley began to play Chopin for the company, no doubt so she wouldn't be forced to join the curious crowd around Emmie. Emmie accepted dozens of expressions of congratulations and good wishes from the lady guests. She tried her best to answer Ottoline's numerous inquiries about her family, the wedding date, the site of the wedding, and who was to be invited. Finally she was able to get away for a walk around the room, claiming that she'd been seated too long for her comfort.

To restore her good mood, Emmie admired the

coffered ceiling with its recessed panels. Each had a powder blue background and gilded stucco decoration. Within the panels had been painted mythological scenes. She looked around for any spiral motifs, but this room had been redecorated in the eighteenth century by Robert Adam.

If old Beaufort had hidden his traitor's gold here, the clue to its location had been lost. This thought darkened Emmie's humor, and it didn't improve when the gentlemen invaded the salon. North joined her immediately, took her hand, and placed it on his arm.

When she tried to remove it, he placed his hand over hers and murmured with a smile, "Remember our agreement. You're besotted with me."

Wishing she could kick him in the shins, Emmie gave him a counterfeit smile.

"I hope your face freezes in that nasty grin," she said.

"Now, my dear," North said in a loud voice. "You mustn't dote on me so. If you begin this way, I shall be terribly spoiled even before we're married."

"You bloody—ow!" Emmie hissed at him. "Stop pinching me, you vile hypocrite, or I swear by the saints I'll black your eye."

"Lower your voice and smile, dammit."

Emmie bit her lip, then beamed at Aunt Ottoline as the older woman joined them. "Dear Lady Ottoline."

"Do call me Aunt, my dear. After all, we'll soon be family."

"Dear Aunt, do you know what Valin has just told me? In a few weeks when the guests are gone, he wants to return to London and celebrate our engagement with a wonderful finish to the Season. Lots and lots of balls and dinners and parties and musicals. He wants you to plan as many as possible, with hundreds of guests."

North dropped her hand. "What!"

"Oh, my." Ottoline stared at her nephew with wonder and gratitude. "How marvelous, Valin. I'm so pleased you're going to allow me to help you introduce your fiancée in this manner. You and Emily will be the toast of London if I have anything to do with it. Now let me see. We'll open with a ball, and we'll see if we can't persuade the Queen and Prince Albert to come, although they almost never do."

While Ottoline chattered Emmie pretended to listen, beaming at Valin.

North was shaking his head. "Now, Aunt, I'm not sure—"

"Don't worry about a thing, my dear," Ottoline said. "I'll do all the planning. Oh, I shall be of use to you at last."

North's lips stretched, revealing white teeth in

what was supposed to be a pleased smile and ended up resembling the grimace of an enraged lion.

"How generous of you, Aunt. And now if you'll excuse us, I promised Emily I'd take her for a walk in the gardens. She wanted to see the maze in moonlight."

"No, I don't," Emily said quickly.

"Nonsense, my dear. Aunt won't mind at all, and it's proper now that we're to be married."

Emmie felt his hand grip her arm hard, and she was steered outside through the tall French windows that opened onto a stone terrace. Once they were out of sight of the salon, North sped up and dragged her after him as he went down the long flight of stairs to the Elizabethan maze. Tall yews had been cut in a complex pattern in which guests were continually losing themselves. Emmie trotted after her captor, pulling back only to be yanked forward as they darted into the labyrinth. After a few twists and turns, she was lost in the darkness.

She grabbed a thick branch and dug in her heels. "Release me."

North turned, plucked her hand from the branch, and tugged her after him without a word. Suddenly the yews opened and they were in a court lit with moonbeams.

Emmie tried to pry North's fingers from her wrist, but without warning he dragged her against

him, capturing her arms and lifting her until her
eyes were level with his.

"You broke your promise, Emily No-name.
And I'm grateful, because now I can show you
what happens to a naughty lady adventuress who
doesn't keep her word."

9

Valin felt Emily de Winter tremble as he drew her closer. The shivering penetrated his arms. No, no, it was he who was shivering! Valin stopped trying to pull the struggling young woman to him as he realized how little mastery he had over himself. When he stopped, she quit fighting him and remained still, catching her breath. She was close enough for him to see her softly curved face bathed in silver moonlight, and he forgot his ire.

"Peace?" he whispered. She said nothing.

For long moments they stayed as they were, each waiting for the other to do something. Valin watched the patterns of moonbeam and shadow formed by the yews play over her face and illuminate the pearls in her hair. The distraction didn't help him in his fight for control. Somehow he found himself bending toward her. She watched him warily, but didn't move.

He was closing the space between them, but it seemed to take him hours. Every second he expected her to bolt. Even when his lips touched hers he expected her to push him back, but her body melted into his, and he wrapped his arms around her as he explored her mouth.

In spite of the barrier of gown and corset he sensed when her breathing quickened and grew ragged. She caught him off guard when she responded to his kiss by hooking her arms around his neck and lifting herself to him, pressing her mouth to his and chasing his tongue with hers. Suddenly it was she who led and he who responded. On fire now, Valin slid his hand to the neck of her gown.

At this touch, Emily uttered a strangled cry deep in her throat, tore her lips from his, and sprang out of his grasp. As she moved she thrust him away. The abrupt change was a shock. Valin stumbled and caught himself before he fell, but Emily was already halfway across the court.

Desperate to mask his frustration and disappointment, Valin laughed. "Where are you going, Miss No-name? You don't know the way out."

"I've gotten out of plenty of rum spots, and this place doesn't compare!"

He heard a swish of skirts, and she was gone. Valin allowed her a minute to get lost, then went after her. This time his grin was anticipatory. He'd never had to literally chase a woman before, and it was exciting. Rushing out of the court, he hurried to the first dead end. She wasn't there. He tried the next, but only startled a nightingale. Bursting into a run, he chased after a sound he thought was Emily. By the time he reached the next dead end, he was lost. It was too dark, and he hadn't paid attention to where he was going.

"Damn."

In answer to his exclamation he heard a light laugh, the rustle of silk, and the click of slipper heels as Miss Emily de Winter walked unhurriedly back to the house.

He called after her in a loud whisper. "Come back here at once." He listened intently. "Emily? Dammit, woman, where are you?"

He heard her shut the terrace doors in response. She'd left him out here. Curse the girl. She knew he'd gotten turned around, and she'd left him to stumble about in the dark, the little beast.

With resignation, Valin began to backtrack, trying to find a familiar path among the yews. As he walked, he grinned to himself. Matching wits with Emily de Winter was much more fun than spending time with any other woman he'd known.

"Fun," he said to himself.

He hardly ever used that word. It was an Acton word, a Courtland word, even, but not one of his words. His words were duty, responsibility, honor. His days were filled with such words and their corresponding obligations. His responsibilities had been drilled into him as long as he could remember.

Once he'd known how to have fun. He could remember being young and in love with the feeling he got from climbing high in an ancient oak and allowing his body to be carried with the sway of the branches in the wind. He and Acton had played tricks on their governess, Miss Ickleton. Once they'd put a hedgehog into the foot of her bed beneath the covers. Another time he'd put a frog in the poor woman's bonnet while it was hanging on a peg. Acton had rolled on the floor, weak with laughter at the sight of their dignified governess with a frog on her head. Luckily Miss Ickleton had possessed a sense of humor.

When had he given up fun? Not long after the frog incident, when he was eight, his father and mother began impressing upon him the nature of his duties and responsibilities as heir. From then on, all his actions, all his words were judged by those standards.

His mother's favorite phrase became, "Such conduct is unworthy of your father's heir."

Father was more direct.

"A Marquess of Westfield does not whine, sir," he would say. Or, "The Westfield heir knows how to sit a horse, sir, and he doesn't do it like a coster-monger out for a country treat."

Being heir had ruined fun, that was certain. No wonder Acton scoffed at him. No wonder laughing with Miss de Winter made him feel as if he was coming back to life after having been dead for twenty years.

Even more invigorating was her mysteriousness. Society had no members whose names were unknown, and he'd never met a woman of breeding with such a vocabulary. What epithets might she use if he made her truly angry? The prospect was intriguing, but he wasn't going to gain Miss de Winter's cooperation by making her furious. That much he learned tonight. Could he gain it by more subtle methods, more honey than horseradish?

Valin found the center court of the maze at last and began to retrace the way out. Perhaps he'd find out more about his fiancée by making her his friend and ally. He didn't want a repeat of her behavior this evening, that was certain. There was no telling what misery she might cause him if he made her angry enough. Already he was committed to returning to London to finish the Season. The thought was enough to make him want to howl at the moon.

Stepping out of the maze, Valin caught a glimpse of Emily through the French doors. She was laughing with Acton and Courtland in the center of a pool of golden light from a chandelier. For a brief moment she seemed a creature of enchantment—unreachable, ephemeral, elusive, casting spells upon all who came within her province. Then she turned her head and looked outside, and he could have sworn she knew he was there looking at her.

Was she so magical that she could sense him across such a distance? While others talked around her, she gazed into the night, a slight smile playing on her lips. He remained where he was, hoping urgently that she would leave his brothers and come to him and make this imaginary enchantment real.

The spell was broken when Acton bowed to her. Emily turned and allowed him to lead her away from the window. Valin let out his breath; he hadn't realized he'd been holding it. He rolled his shoulders to rid them of the tension that had built up simply from beholding Miss Emily de Winter. This wouldn't do. He had to break free of these foolish notions she put in his head merely by coming near him.

He would try to make peace with her. Perhaps they'd become friends. So mundane a relationship would banish these fancies. One didn't lust after a friend. He couldn't indulge in absurd imaginings about someone he hardly knew, who was, after all, a common adventuress, however well mannered.

That was the answer. He and Emily would settle into a friendly arrangement that would allow her to tell him the truth about herself. Once the puzzle of Miss de Winter had been solved, he could get on with his search for a suitable wife. There would be no distraction of a young woman veiled in mystery. No longer would she intrigue him with her exotic behavior, her wildness, and her courage.

Valin nodded to himself. Once he knew her secrets, he would no longer want her so unbearably. He began to walk toward the house. Best start immediately, tomorrow morning. Before Miss de Winter had time to get him into more trouble than she already had.

❧

The next morning Valin stayed behind when the rest of his gentlemen guests went shooting. He was on his way to the archery butts that had been set up on the lawn stretching between the gardens and the park behind Agincourt. He was hurrying down the terrace stairs when Acton called his name and came running after him from the house.

"I want to talk to you," he said.

Valin waved him away. "I've already arranged to settle all your debts."

"It's not about that."

Valin sighed and gazed over the balustrade that separated the next terrace from the formal gardens and the yew maze. It was a cool May morning that wore a coat of silver dew and new leaves. He was sure Acton would spoil it.

"About this engagement," Acton said. "Are you mad?"

"What do you mean?"

"We know nothing of this Miss de Winter. We don't know her parents."

"They're dead." Valin could see the ladies aiming at the archery targets.

"Or her people."

He couldn't see Miss de Winter. "They live in France and in Northumberland."

"And her face and fortune are mediocre," Acton said.

Valin dragged his gaze from the archers to stare at his brother. "Are you maligning the young woman I've asked to be my wife?"

"I'm surprised, that's all. And you have to admit there are dozens of girls much prettier and richer."

"She has enough money to suit me, and I think she's lovely. Of what possible interest could either matter be to you?" Valin narrowed his eyes and said quietly, "Ah, I see. You'd rather be marquess yourself, but if I'm to be it, then you want me to marry someone whose fortune will serve as a reserve bank for you."

Acton flushed. "That's a damned lie."

"Then you're concerned for my future happiness? How touching."

"I just don't see why you're in such a hurry to get married," Acton snapped. "You weren't before, and I know why."

Valin rounded on his brother. "Be careful, Acton."

"You were afraid no woman would have you. You were afraid the old rumors would start again. Have any of them asked you about—"

"Shut up, will you?"

"Are you going to tell Miss de Winter?" Acton sauntered around Valin, a quizzical look on his face. "Or would you like me to do it, since you never like to talk about it? I could, you know. I'll say to her, Oh, by the way, Miss de Winter, pay no attention to the silly rumor that my brother burned our father and stepmother to death in the old lodge when he was seventeen."

Acton held up a finger. "And there's no truth to the rumor that he seduced my stepmother. No truth to it at all. Those fights between him and my father were over boyish pranks at school, not over dear Carolina. Not at all." Acton stood grinning nastily at Valin.

"You are a bastard, aren't you?" Valin said.

"I'm only offering to help you, old fellow."

Not trusting himself, Valin went down the terrace steps, then stopped. "Acton, do you remember the last time we had a fight? A physical one, that is."

"Yes."

"Do you remember who won?"

Acton scowled at him.

"If you speak ill of me to Miss de Winter, you'll spend the rest of the Season in bed recovering from our next fight."

He left the terrace swiftly, fearing he'd lose control and tie Acton's legs around his neck. Acton had a talent for ferreting out one's weaknesses and using them as weapons. Valin had learned not to let his brother see that his barbs drew blood, but this attack had been so unexpected that he'd lost his temper. The old memories flooded his senses, and he was seeing images over a decade old.

Father had been married to Carolina for several years, and that day he'd gone to a neighbor's to see about the purchase of a Thoroughbred. It was high summer, one of those hot, bright days when the heat bakes flies into a stupor and insects sing to the sun. He was home from school for a few weeks and had been riding that morning. Arriving home, he found a note from Carolina asking him to meet her at the old lodge.

Carolina made him nervous. She was only eight years his senior, but she had an air of experience about her. When they were in each other's company Carolina would fix him with an appraising look that made him turn red. His confusion never failed to gratify her.

What was worse, she had a habit of making embarrassing remarks under her breath, making sure only he heard them. Once, before dinner, they'd been alone in the drawing room, and he'd knelt to stoke the fire. Suddenly she was beside him on the floor with her hand on his thigh. He'd nearly fallen on his ass scrambling to get away from her.

Why was she at the lodge? He had no desire to meet her there to become the mouse in her game of hunting cat. Valin tossed the note in the wastebasket in his room, but hesitated as he started to remove his riding coat. The last time he'd refused to see Carolina she'd complained of his rudeness to Father. If he displeased her, it would only end in unpleasantness. Perhaps he should meet her and come to some understanding; if he made it clear to her that he was unwilling to play games with her, there would be less trouble all around.

Valin pulled his jacket back on, returned to the stables, and was soon riding through the park. The old lodge was a hunting box built by an ancestor when King James was a frequent visitor to Agincourt Hall. Its red brick facade concealed an interior gloomy with dark wood paneling. The narrow windows had been enlarged, but their diamond-shaped panes still kept out too much light. It was used infrequently, and Valin disliked its tiny rooms and numerous drafts. The place was so dark and cold that one had to light candles and keep the fireplace running even on a summer day.

Upon reaching the lodge, Valin knocked but received no answer. He went inside to find the rooms on the ground floor deserted. With growing irritation he realized Carolina had probably forgotten her summons and wasn't even here.

Then he heard her laugh. He was about to call to her when he heard her again. This time she was singing to herself. Valin followed the sound upstairs, but his steps slowed when he recognized the tune. It was a bawdy tavern song with which no lady should have been familiar. As he hesitated, a silence fell.

Anxious to get this interview over with, Valin hurried across the landing to a half-open door. His fist was raised to knock on the portal when Carolina's voice reached him.

"Come in, Valin. I've been waiting much too long."

He recognized that teasing, suggestive tone. Torn between leaving at once and the need to placate his stepmother, Valin went into the room. Carolina was standing in the middle of the chamber wrapped in a brocade dressing gown. She had lit a fire and placed dozens of candles around a four-poster bed. She gave him a little mincing smile and opened her dressing gown.

Valin's mouth was already open. Now his eyes widened to the size of dessert plates and blood rushed to his head. Confusion and horror burned through Valin's mind while his body turned into glacial ice. He couldn't speak or move.

"My sweet, sweet Valin," Carolina purred, "at last you're here."

Valin gawked at her as she sauntered over to him. Surveying him from head to foot. The pupils of her eyes were dilated, and she slurred her words slightly.

"I had an argument with myself," she said. "The good Carolina said to wait. After all, you haven't even been to university yet. But naughty Carolina had a fit. She's so, so anxious, you see. And naughty Carolina won."

Valin swallowed hard as she stood in front of him, hands on her bare hips, the dressing gown hanging from her arms and trailing behind her.

"Come, Valin. Say something instead of standing there looking like a stunned buck."

His mouth dry, his body stiff, Valin felt as if he was separate from the scene being played. He watched as Carolina took his hand and placed it on her breast. That touch jolted him out of his daze.

He shoved Carolina away and turned to leave, but she quickly twisted him around and sank her hand into his hair, pulling his face toward her. Her mouth was almost touching his before he was able to disentangle himself and back away. She came after him, and he sped up to avoid her grasp. Her grin should have warned him, but he lost his balance before he realized he'd backed into the bed.

His stepmother was there as he landed. Slipping a knee between his legs, she placed her hands on his shoulders and shoved him deep into the mattress. Alarmed, Valin freed one arm and tried to get a grip on the woman. Suddenly he felt something around his wrist. His arm was jerked, and he realized Carolina had tied a leather thong around his wrist and attached it to a bedpost. Stunned, he watched as she slipped another thong around his other wrist.

"Be still, lover," Carolina said. "You're going to like this."

"No!"

Valin bucked and yanked against the thongs— but they held. Carolina had apparently done this before.

Now she was breathing hard from their struggles, but her humor remained. "I should have taken more time with you, my pretty. But I do so like a man with a little fight in him."

When Valin tried to free his arms again she slid

on top of him, slipped her hand under his shirt and found his waist. Valin tried to shake her off, but he couldn't prevent her from moving her hand between his legs. When she squeezed him gently, he let out a roar of outrage and lunged up, off the bed. This time Carolina toppled to the floor with him. One of Valin's wrists was still tethered to the bedpost, but the violence of their struggle had wrenched the frame apart. One post crashed against a bedside table, sending a candelabrum skidding to hit the far wall, where floor-length curtains framed a window.

Fighting to free his bound wrist, Valin had no time to escape when Carolina pounced on him again. She took his mouth in a violent kiss. Then, out of the corner of his eye, he glimpsed the flames. He tried to speak, but Carolina's tongue was in his mouth. Desperate, Valin stopped trying to fight her and concentrated on freeing himself from the broken bedpost. While her hands roamed over him, invading and arousing a response he couldn't control, Valin tried to untie the leather thong. It had been jerked even tighter by the fall.

Without warning, Carolina released his mouth. "There's a fire, damn you!" he cried.

She wasn't listening. Her gaze caressed the flames, and to his horror Valin realized the danger had only excited her more. She looked down at him and tore his shirt open.

"You make me burn as hot as the fire."

Valin's body tensed with a strength he hadn't possessed before, and the thong snapped. Leaping up, he sprang away from her.

"Come on. We have to get out."

She pulled her bedraggled dressing gown around her shoulders as the flames jumped from the curtains to the bed. "Just a few minutes, pretty one. We have that much time, and it will be so good with the fire almost on us."

Valin's stream of curses was cut short when flames shot across the ceiling. In less than a second the wall by the door was ablaze. Carolina didn't seem to care, and Valin realized she was either drunk or had taken some drug.

But the crackle and roar of the fire spurred Valin. "Come now, damn it!"

He worked his way across the room and hurtled through the flames that surrounded the door. Once outside, he found that his stepmother hadn't followed him. Carolina stood where he'd left her. He yelled for her to hurry. Something of his desperation must have reached her at last. Gathering her dressing gown around her, she rushed toward him, but the fire shot across the carpet and into her skirts.

Valin tried to go back, but the searing heat blocked him. Fire burned his clothes. He could hear Carolina screaming as he stumbled back, coughing. In desperation, he ran downstairs for water. There was an old pump in the kitchen yard. Valin grabbed a bucket and filled it, but by the time he got to the stairs the fire had spread to the landing. He could still hear his stepmother screaming.

Horrified, Valin rushed outside again, this time to his horse. He had his foot in the stirrup when his father galloped up, shouting at him.

"What's happened?"

His throat hoarse, lungs burned, Valin gasped out, "Carolina is in there. We've got to get help!"

They stared at each other for a terrible moment, then his father was gone. Valin sprang after him, catching him only at the front door.

"You can't go in there," he said. "It's too dangerous."

His father shrugged him off, but he caught the older man again. This time, without a word, his father spun around and clipped Valin on the chin. Valin hit the ground swimming in pain, then blacked out. When he regained consciousness he was in the midst of a milling crowd, and the entire lodge was aflame. Valin struggled to his feet and stumbled toward it, but two men held him back. As he fought them, a figure carrying another person appeared at one of the upper windows. Or was it his imagination?

Valin screamed and pointed, but no one else saw. "Let me go, damn you, he's there!"

"We don't see nothin', and it don't matter, sir. Whoever's in there is for it. Jesus, Billie, help me with him."

Valin tried to hit one of his captors, and got a punch to the jaw that sent him into blackness once again.

The darkness dissolved, as did the years, and Valin returned to the present to find himself standing in the middle of the lawn. The ladies had noticed him and were calling. He managed to wave and smile as he trudged toward them.

Acton had been right. He was mad to consider marriage. What woman of virtue and honor would want to marry a murderer?

10

❧❧❧

The morning after she'd left Valin floundering in the yew maze, Emmie sat beside Courtland in his study in the Gallery Tower. Underneath her tranquil exterior—while she listened to her host and nodded with interest—her entire being vibrated with turmoil. If she'd been piano wire she would have popped loose and zinged across the room. Last night she'd set out to cause the marquess trouble, and she'd succeeded. It had been exciting to provoke him out of his stern and masterful complacency.

And then she'd lost her wits in the yew maze. Valin North had driven her mad with anger and temptation at the same time, and she had grown so confused that she actually allowed him to kiss her. No, she had kissed him. Gracious mercy, what a kiss. A few more moments of that kind of kissing, and she would have ended up on the ground with him, making the yews shake.

Dear heaven. She hadn't known kissing could be like that, hadn't suspected what it could lead to. If Betsy ever found out, she'd laugh. All her friends would snicker and tease her for falling under the spell of an accomplished seducer like the marquess. How humiliating.

Everyone had heard stories about Valin and the Countess of Maxa, and Lady Perdita Strangeways, and Mrs. George William Arbuthnot. How dare he try to add her to that list?

She had to put Valin North in his proper place in her head—that of a rich dupe. But try as she might, he refused to remain in this safe category. She was desperate to hide that fact from her friends, and she longed to hide it from herself as well, but the truth was that Valin North was no dupe, and certainly not her prey. Indeed, it seemed that the moment she got near him her prey turned into a predator, one she feared she might not be able to resist.

The solution was to put him out of her thoughts. She ought to feel quite satisfied this morning, because she'd found a way to get into the Gallery Tower without arousing suspicion. She'd befriended Courtland North, and it was to his studies that many of the rooms in the tower were dedicated. The young man had been flustered by her attention at first, then heartbreakingly grateful to find a lady who wanted to listen to him.

Another reason for her to be satisfied was unexpected. She was wearing a prim gown chosen specially for this visit with Valin's brother. It was a high-necked day dress of dusky blue. Made of soft chambray with a lace collar, it had graceful flared sleeves and undersleeves of embroidered muslin.

In her real life she'd never wear anything so delicate during the day, certainly not in the streets of St. Giles. Wearing this soft and impractical gown in daytime, here, in a clean, paneled room filled with books, made her feel more like a lady than wearing the finest ball gown. Betsy had rolled her eyes when she helped Emmie dress, and Emmie knew her friend thought she'd worn the gown for the marquess. The idea was absurd.

Emmie sternly remembered her purpose. After this lay was over, the gowns would be sold and the money added to her savings for the children.

To befriend Valin's brother, she'd persuaded him that she shared his interest in things medieval. This ruse would afford her a glimpse of the rooms he used in the Gallery and an excuse to wander into the tower later.

The young man had been chattering for a quarter hour about his latest purchase. Emmie had but to nod once in a while and exclaim a few times.

Then he was off again on another explanation. All the while Emmie darted glances about Courtland's document room in search of spirals. The chamber had been made over by Beaufort shortly before his arrest, and she had great hopes for it.

"I know you'll appreciate this." Courtland rose and opened a glass case with hushed reverence.

Emmie joined him. Within the case rested a large illuminated parchment. Knowing nothing about it, Emmie feigned amazement.

"Do tell me about this marvel, Lord Courtland."

"It's the full achievement of William, fourth Marquess of Winchester. Look at the first quarter of the shield. It shows Paulet Sable, three swords in pile, points downward, Argent pommels, and hilts Or. Isn't it magnificent?"

"Argent pommels," Emmie breathed. "Amazing."

"I knew you'd appreciate the artistry."

"Oh, indeed." Emmie examined the paneling behind the document case, but she found no decoration. The wood in this room seemed free of almost any carving beyond the Beaufort arms.

"Miss de Winter, are you listening?"

"Of course," Emmie replied as she turned back to Courtland with a smile. "You were talking about the animals used to make up heraldic devices."

Courtland beamed at her. "Yes. It's quite simple, you know. In the thirteenth century, for example, rolls of arms include barbels, lucies—which are pike—and hake, for the families of Bar, Lucy, and Hacket."

"That makes wonderful sense." Emmie ran her hand over a Tudor period chest in which Courtland stored some of his reference books. "Why don't you show me that chimneypiece with the Beaufort achievement carved on it."

"Do you really want to see it?" Courtland looked past her and smiled. "There you are. We've been having the most fascinating conversation."

Emmie whirled around, suspecting the worst. She was right. Valin North stood in the doorway. What was he doing here? Had he discovered her true object in coming to Agincourt Hall? She watched him warily as he came into the room with that slow, graceful walk that reminded her of a king going to his coronation in Westminster Abbey. He drew near, took her hand, and kissed it. Emmie withdrew it as soon as she could, and ignored the way her body tingled even after his touch was gone.

"Hello, Courtland old fellow. I went looking for my dear Miss de Winter and couldn't find her, until the ladies told me you'd abducted her."

Courtland was already reading one of his books. "What? Oh, well, Miss de Winter is the only young lady here who has sense enough to appreciate history. Did you know she's interested in the Elizabethan period? She knows all about old Beaufort and his troubles with Queen Bess."

"Does she?"

Emmie looked away when Valin regarded her with a skeptical expression.

"I was going to show her the Beaufort chimneypiece upstairs, but now you're here, you can do it. I want to find that record of the visitation by Windsor Herald. It was in that lot you let me buy a few weeks ago, and it's from this county in 1588, the year of the Armada. Miss de Winter especially wanted to see it."

Emmie glanced at Valin's severe expression. "I'm not in a hurry, Courtland. We'll wait for you."

"Nonsense," Valin said as he gripped her arm and steered her out of the room. "Old Courtland will get distracted by some rotting battle standard or a bestiary, and we'll never see the damned chimneypiece."

Once the door shut on his brother Valin released Emmie. "What are you doing?"

"Whatever do you mean, my lord?" He'd found her out. Nothing to do but face him.

"You're hiding from me."

Emmie stared at him blankly. "Me, hide from you?" She laughed with nervous relief.

Valin snatched her wrist and bent down to her eye level.

"Then why are you pretending to be interested in Courtland's studies? All the young ladies avoid him as if he were a leper."

Yanking her hand free, Emmie straightened her flared sleeves. "If they do, they're stupid and insensitive. Anyone can see your brother is intelligent and sweet-tempered and perceptive." Emmie glanced up from her sleeve. "And it would take more than a bullying nobleman to make me hide."

"You're serious."

Emmie merely lifted her brows. Valin glanced at the closed door, then offered his arm. After a moment's hesitation, Emmie placed her hand on it, and they walked upstairs. She wasn't going to let him think she was afraid to be alone with him. He opened a door set in a pointed arch, and with a sweep of his arm ushered Emmie inside another tower room.

This chamber had a series of tall windows with pointed arches of the same design as the one over the door. Through them Emmie saw a wide swath of sky, the park, and wooded hills that rolled to the horizon. The windows had been opened, and a breeze played with her skirts. Emmie forgot her nervousness.

Captivated by the airiness of the room and the contrast between the azure sky and forest green of the hills, Emmie hurried to one of the windows. Outside the world was clean. In St. Giles everything from the roofs to the cobbles was covered with damp soot and grime from coal fires and the myriad industrial processes that went on in the city.

For days at a time London was shrouded in a choking yellow fog. When the fog retreated, bright sunshine only served to reveal the dinginess of Emmie's surroundings. She leaned out the window and breathed in air free of coal and gas fumes and the stench of filth. She was going to hate returning to London.

"I'm sorry."

Emmie started and hit her head on the window. "Bloody damnation!" She pressed her hand to her head and allowed Valin to guide her away from the window.

"My apologies again, Miss de Winter."

"Wasn't your fault," Emmie mumbled as she rubbed her head. "I was thinking of something else."

"What?"

"How much nicer it is here than in London."

"I agree," Valin said as he sat down next to her on the bench in front of the window. "That's why I stay here rather than in town most of the time. But I wanted to apologize for mistaking your intentions toward my brother. You see, you're one of the few women who has ever appreciated him."

He smiled at her, and Emmie felt her heart start to do that disturbing polka again. She felt the corners of her mouth wander upward, and before she knew it she was smiling back at him. For a tyrant, Valin North took a deal of trouble over a reclusive younger brother.

His smile faded a bit, and became rueful. "I just wish I could lure old Courtland away from his studies for a while."

Emmie shrugged. "Why should he leave them when he isn't wanted?"

"What do you mean? I want him. I've tried many times to get him to do something else."

"Why?"

Valin gave an exasperated sigh. "To give him other interests. So I can spend some time with him."

"Why?"

"Because he's my brother," Valin snapped.

"And?"

Valin scowled at her, but Emmie folded her arms and waited.

"And?" Valin repeated.

"He's your brother, and . . ."

Valin gave her a confused look, and Emmie threw up her hands.

"And you love him! Did you ever say that to him?" she asked.

"Of course not," Valin said. "A chap doesn't go around saying things like that."

"Why not?"

Thrusting himself off the bench, Valin stalked away from her while running a hand through his hair in exasperation. "Because he's a chap, that's why."

"Oh, I see. *Chaps* don't love their brothers."

Valin rounded on her. "That's not what I meant, and you know it. Miss de Winter, I find this subject most inappropriate. Look at the chimneypiece."

She'd forgotten again! Gracious mercy, she lost all sense when this man was around. She looked down at her hands. They were trembling! When had they started trembling? It was when he'd thrust his fingers through his hair. That soft mahogany hair. God deliver her from beautiful tyrants.

Resolutely Emmie banished all hot and unmanageable thoughts from her head. She rose and went to stand beside Valin before the fireplace. The massive facing over the fireplace went from floor to ceiling, and the armorial bearings of old Henry Beaufort were carved over the mantel. Emmie glanced at the shield surmounted by the coronet of rank, but while Valin described the coat of arms, her gaze fell to the frieze decorating the front of the mantel and stuck there.

Spirals. Dozens of spirals carved into the Italian marble. In the chimneypiece put here by Henry Beaufort shortly before he was arrested for treason. Shortly after he'd received all that lovely Spanish treasure.

"What's wrong, Emily?" Valin asked.

"Nothing, nothing's wrong. What could be wrong? There's nothing wrong."

"Then why are you babbling?"

Emmie tore her gaze from the spirals only to meet his gentle regard. Gone was the irascible frown. Instead she found a gaze that seemed bemused and entranced, and Emmie was caught off guard.

She couldn't look away. She wanted to. She wanted to escape this feeling of standing exposed on a hill while great thunderclouds filled with lightning rolled toward her. One of her feet lifted seemingly of its own accord, and she'd almost forced it to step back when he said her name again.

If only he hadn't said her name in that rough-gentle way he had. If only he would move away so that she didn't feel his warmth or hear the way his breathing speeded up. If only he hadn't spoken again. But he did, in that intimate whisper that seemed to wind a steel spring inside her tighter and tighter.

"I don't want to fight with you, Emmie." He lifted her hand to his lips. "Can't we have peace between us?"

"I don't know." Her mouth was dry, and if he didn't stop kissing the back of her hand she'd scream. "If you don't stop kissing the back of my hand, I'll scream."

Emmie clapped her free hand over her mouth, but the words were out, and Valin was smiling at her. Only this smile was one she'd seen before. It was a smile at home in ladies' bedrooms, in haystacks with farm girls, and in closets with parlor maids. Emmie felt her cheeks burn. She pulled her hand out of his grasp and scurried for the door. She nearly ran into him when he blocked her way.

Careening backward, she said, "Stay where you are."

"Nonsense. I want to make you scream."

He stalked toward her like a duelist. She retreated, desperate to regain her composure.

"I shan't scream unless you fail to remain where you are."

"Oh, Emmie. We both know you're not going to scream. Not yet."

Emmie's foot hit a baseboard, and she sidled along the wall. "We know nothing of the kind. I— I'll do more than scream."

He stopped then. Emmie stared at him, and wished she didn't feel so cheated now that he was immobile. Drawing herself up, she nodded to him and walked toward the door. As she passed him, he slipped an arm around her waist and pulled her close.

"Bloody h—" The word was smothered by his mouth.

Emmie began to struggle, but he lifted his mouth just enough to whisper, "Don't, my love."

Valin moved his head back, and they stared at each other. To Emmie it seemed as if that one word froze him, but he lowered his mouth to hers so quickly she wasn't sure if she'd imagined that fleeting, startled look in his eyes. Love. That one word stunned her. It was a word she seldom heard, and never had a man used it in reference to her. Such thoughts clamored in her head, but the insistence of his mouth drew her into a whirlpool of heat and pressure and intensity. His hands pressed against her back; his fingers traced designs of fire on her ribs, and her breasts were crushed against his chest.

In moments Emmie's own hands began a fevered exploration of their own until they found bare flesh. She touched a mound of muscle over his shoulder as her gown loosened and fell around her waist. His mouth traveled from her neck to her breast as he bent her back over one arm. Emmie gasped at the feel of his lips, but her world of fire and frenzy exploded when she heard Courtland's voice.

"Miss de Winter?"

Almost dizzy, she made no protest when Valin immediately left her, slipped through the door, and closed it. She heard the men's voices outside. Evidently Courtland had found a volume of Elizabethan history for her. She listened to Valin as he redirected his brother's attention. Then she noticed that her hair was falling around her bare shoulders. She looked down at herself.

"Bloody damnation!"

With shaking hands she pulled her gown over her shoulders and tried to fasten the buttons in back. It was impossible after the first three, so she dropped to her knees and began gathering hairpins.

"Gracious mercy, what have I done? Gracious mercy." It was the yew maze all over again. Lost wits and agitated body, these were her downfall.

She heard the door open and close, and heavy steps behind her, but she refused to turn around. That was a mistake, because Valin dropped to the floor beside her, grabbed her shoulders, and kissed her. Emmie felt his fingers exploring her naked back and cried out. She pushed him and jumped to her feet.

"No!"

"Now, Emmie."

"I said no," she said, and she rushed to the door.

Valin chuckled and stood up. "You can't leave with your dress falling around your waist and your hair down."

Twisting around, Emmie put her back against the door and watched him with distrust. She might look disheveled, but he looked wild. He was breathing heavily and his eyes looked like sterling silver in the sun's glare. He was coming toward her! Emmie put her hand on the door latch. Valin stopped and lifted his arms away from his body in a gesture of conciliation.

"I'll be a gentleman."

"I don't trust you."

Valin lowered his arms. "Emmie, my dear, you have three choices. You can leave in your present state and be disgraced, or you can allow me to fasten your clothing and straighten your hair. Or you can fight me as you're doing now, in which case we'll end up on the floor and more than your gown will be ruined."

Only moments ago he'd used the word love. Had he meant it? Or did he use the word as a common term of endearment to ladies he desired? Emmie blinked rapidly and tried to think, but she had no experience in real love. In her many deceptions her victims had declared worship, affection, yet she'd always recognized the illusion. Now she wasn't sure.

Once she'd played a governess for a few weeks to discover the plan of a house. Its owner had tried to seduce her behind his wife's back. That wasn't love, and it had reminded her of her mother's tragedy. As a French comtesse she'd dallied in society for brief periods during which many men had paid her attentions and made illicit proposals. That wasn't love.

She was convinced that what her mother felt for Edmund Cheap couldn't have been love. She loved Flash, Phoebe, and Sprout. She loved Dolly and Betsy and Turnip and Pilfer. There had never been the time or the chance to love anyone else.

Hesitating, with reluctance and cold palms, Emmie went to Valin and turned her back to him. "Please fasten my buttons."

She felt his hands on her gown for a moment. Then they lifted without having fastened the buttons, and she turned around to find him staring at his fingers. He looked up, his face devoid of any anger or severity. His eyes were wide with astonishment.

"My hands are shaking."

"I was shaking all over when I heard Courtland."

"No, you don't understand. They weren't shaking until—"

"Yes?"

Emmie waited, but Valin only shook his head and turned her around. This time he fastened her gown. When she began to restore the arrangement of her hair, he helped her lift the heavy curls in place at the back of her head. She handed him the last pin, and he slipped it into place. His hand remained on the hair gathered into its neat coil.

"Upon my soul," he whispered.

She turned her head. "What's wrong?"

"I don't know," he said absently. His hands came down to rest on her shoulders, and his lips hovered near her ear. "Emmie, what have you done to me?"

Twisting around, Emmie cried, "Me? I've done nothing. You're the wicked one, kissing me and— and undoing my—and making me—Oh!"

He was grinning at her in such a knowing manner that Emmie turned red again and blurted out, "I'll not stay here to be crowed over by you, my lord."

She picked up her skirts and marched to the door. Yanking it open, she swept through it majestically. Between chuckles, Valin responded.

"Don't go, my dear. If you stay we'll have more kissing and undoing, and I know you'll like it just as much as before."

"I'd rather spend a week with muck snipes, lags,

and mutchers, or take my chances with the crushers, than stay another minute with you!"

She was about to shut the door when his voice came to her again, this time as soft as the breeze that still played with her skirts.

"Emmie."

Her gaze locked with his.

"Please don't leave me."

Something flickered in his eyes, and he held out his hand to her. The sight of him standing there alone, so tall and perfect, was more frightening than the most fearsome underworld enemy.

"I can't stay," she said.

"Why not?"

She only stared at him, and he went on. "We have to talk."

"No, we don't. We have an agreement, my lord. Please adhere to it and keep away from me."

As she closed the door, she heard him say to himself, "Oh, Emmie, you do ask the impossible, don't you."

❧

When she was gone Valin took in a deep breath and let it out, then went to the window to stare out at the tree-covered hills in the distance. A breeze brought the smell of meadow and wildflower. Was it honeysuckle?

Valin shook his head. He had done something just now that he'd never done before. He'd called Emmie "love." The endearment was on his lips before he knew it, slipping out so naturally that at first he thought he'd imagined it. But Emmie's startled look had confirmed his fear. He'd really said it.

And her reaction to him had made him forget the blunder. She desired him as much as he desired her, but she didn't trust him. She was afraid. No doubt the men she usually associated with were untrustworthy. Still, he could see in her eyes the warmth of feeling they shared. They were fond of each other, and they desired each other. He didn't want to think beyond this.

"Don't make that mistake again," Valin said to himself.

He knew why he didn't tell women he loved them. He had avoided the word since Carolina and his father were killed. Father had loved Carolina. For years after the fire he'd been bitter about love, certain that with the emotion came danger, betrayal, unavoidable unhappiness. Women came and went in his life, but he trusted none of them. In the last few years he thought he'd left those foolish and unhappy notions behind, but the word had remained unsaid.

His friends used the word with their wives and mistresses all the time. Until now no woman had

ever provoked in Valin an urge to utter such a dec-
laration. Perhaps the only significance lay in an im-
provement in his disposition brought on by
Emmie's charm.

"Perhaps that's it," he muttered.

Whatever the truth, one thing was certain. He
and Emmie had but to occupy the same room for
attraction to explode between them. Life had suddenly gotten quite interesting.

11

Emmie spent the rest of the day in Aunt Ottoline's company so that she wasn't forced to be alone with Valin again. She needn't have worried, for he was obliged to attend to his other guests. He had to placate the affronted sensibilities of the prospective brides and their families, in addition to smoothing the feathers of dowagers and martinets who found the abrupt announcement lacking in decorum.

The eligible young ladies had packed themselves off, having suddenly found important engagements in town. Miss Kingsley lingered the longest. Emmie had developed a dislike of the young lady, for the way she'd assumed that only she had a chance of attracting and keeping Valin's attention. Until Emmie's engagement had been announced, Miss Kingsley's disdain for her had been apparent.

The evening passed tolerably for Emmie, due to the fact that Acton had invited a few friends of his own for dinner. Their rowdiness and inebriation demanded Valin's constant attention. By the time he was free, Emmie had retired to her rooms where she waited until the Agincourt clocks struck two. Then she and Betsy gathered their workbags and crept through the house to the entrance to the Gallery Tower. There they waited for Turnip and Pilfer.

Lurking in the shadows, Emmie sighed. Betsy set her bag down and crept over to her.

"All right, my girl. What's wrong? You been moping about all day, sighing and goin' about looking like a sick cat."

Emmie mumbled, and Betsy moved closer. "What did you say?"

"I said, the marquess told me he's in love with me."

"Coo!"

"Why would he say it?"

"Don't know. Is he one o' them rum coves that does for the ladies?"

Emmie sighed again. "He's certainly never lacked for their attention, but, well, he's also not one for hiding his irritation or anger at people."

"That's lucky, that is."

"Why?"

"'Cause, stands to reason," Betsy said. "He's the

kind o' bloke who speaks his mind, so he's spoke it to you."

Emmie dared not comment upon this opinion. Betsy was right. Valin North wasn't the kind of man who hid what he thought. If he considered a person a fool, his irritation was apparent in those furious-god scowls of his. Should someone incur his wrath, he was capable of turning his back on him and leaving him in the middle of a gathering to suffer the consequences of social embarrassment. It was reasonable that he'd be equally forthright about his more positive feelings.

"He's never lied to me," Emmie mused.

Betsy snorted. "A rare bloke he is, then."

"But—but now that I've been able to think calmly," Emmie said, "now that I've thought about it . . ."

"Yes?"

"Oh, Betsy." Emmie felt her neck and face grow hot. "I don't know what to think. He called me love at a time when we were—well . . ."

"In one o' them private moments?"

Emmie bit her lip and nodded.

"Hard to say, then."

"And even if he meant it, he doesn't know who I am or what I am or—"

"So? You already said as how he hates all them young ladies what gets thrown at him." Betsy settled against the wall beside the door. "You got a sight more sense than any o' them, and you're lots more interesting."

"I'm not a lady, Betsy. I'm not good enough."

"And them others is?"

Emmie hesitated for a moment. "No."

"Then why not you?" Betsy put her hand on Emmie's arm. "Look, my girl. What's he really got? Besides his blunt and his title I mean. He's got one brother who's a worthless sod, another what buries himself in dusty old books, and an aunt that hasn't got the sense of a hedgehog."

"You mean he's alone."

"Right."

Like me, Emmie thought. Both of us take care of people, but there's no one to take care of us. And when he isn't being scary, he's gentle and almost sweet.

"Look at it this way," Betsy said. "If you don't have him, someone else will, and how are you going to like that? What if he takes up with that prissy Miss Kingsley you're so fond of?"

"That white-livered, pretentious dollymop," Emmie ground out.

"Well, then."

"But he doesn't know who I really am."

"You going to leave here and never see him again?"

Emmie hadn't thought of this. She imagined going back to her old life, a life without the dark-tempered lord who had so changed her. If she'd never met him, she could have returned to London easily. Previously, her occupation and her siblings kept her too busy to notice her loneliness. Now, going back seemed worse than being transported to the wilds of Australia, worse than the treadmill or the workhouse, worse even than Newgate prison. In the past few weeks, her attraction to Valin North had taught her much about her mother's tragedy. Emmie would never have imagined she could be tempted until the devil put Valin in her way. Gracious goodness mercy, what was she going to do?

"They're coming," Betsy whispered.

Emmie heard a gentle clank as Turnip rounded a corner carrying a heavy carpetbag. Pilfer followed him carrying two more empty bags.

"Psst! You there, missus?"

Emmie stepped out of the shadows. "Follow me."

One by one they slipped into the tower and up the winding stair. Emmie made sure everyone tiptoed past Courtland's study and document rooms, as Valin's brother was known to keep late hours when pursuing some fascinating bit of medieval lore. Luckily the rooms were all dark. Emmie found Beaufort's chamber deserted as well, and quickly led her little band to the chimneypiece. Turnip produced a lamp and lit it.

"Coo!" Pilfer cried as he beheld the frieze of spirals. "Where's the treasure?"

"I haven't looked for it yet. Don't be so impatient." Emmie set another lamp on the floor and plucked a scrap of paper from her skirt pocket.

"We might need these."

"Not them foreign words again," Pilfer said.

"They're important." Emmie held the paper to the light. She had translated the four foreign phrases with the help of French and Latin dictionaries.

"Listen. The first phrase is *J'y suis, j'y reste,* 'or 'Here I am, here I remain.'"

She glanced at the others. Turnip shook his head, and Emmie returned to the list. "The rest are in Latin. *'Sic itur ad astra'* means 'Thus one goes to the stars.' Does anyone see any stars?"

"No stars," Betsy said.

Emmie pointed to the next phrase. " '*Si ste viator'* means 'Stop, traveler.' " She exchanged blank looks with her companions and went on. "The fourth phrase is *'Tria juncta in uno.'* That's 'Three joined in one.' Do you see three of anything?" They looked around the room to no avail.

Emmie stuffed the paper back in her pocket. "At least we have the spirals. Perhaps that's all we need. Let's begin."

"Finally," grumbled Pilfer.

Ignoring him, Emmie dropped to her knees,

and Betsy began inspecting the mantel. Turnip started knocking gently on the paneling beside the fireplace. Pilfer squatted near Emmie while she ran her fingertips over the tiles beneath the spiral frieze. There was a loud clank, and they all froze. Turnip sheepishly lifted his foot away from his tool bag and stepped over it. After a few minutes, when it was clear no one was coming to investigate, they resumed their search.

An hour later Emmie stood and blew a tendril of hair off her forehead. "It's not here."

They looked at the chimneypiece.

"Let's stick Pilfer inna chimney," Turnip said.

"Ooo, yes, let me go up."

Emmie shook her head. "It's not in there. Beaufort's paper definitely said the gold was in the chamber under the spiral."

Pilfer kicked one of the empty bags while Betsy packed away the tools they'd used. Shoulders slumped, faces long, they trooped back the way they'd come.

"Coo, this here stair's dark," whispered Pilfer.

"We can't have a light," Emmie replied. "You know we can't take a chance of someone seeing it. Just stay close to the wall so you don't lose your balance."

Turnip's voice seemed loud in the blackness. "What are we going to do now that it's not inna chimney?"

"I'll have to study the clues again," Emmie said. "Those dratted phrases must contain some meaning I haven't discovered. Perhaps I've missed something."

They reached the door to the main house and parted. Emmie went to her room while the others sneaked back into the servants' quarters. Once in bed Emmie admitted to herself that her feelings were more confused than ever.

Part of her was glad she'd be staying awhile longer. If she'd found the gold, she would have absconded despite both Valin's threats and her feelings for him. The money was too important to Flash and the others. But she was staying, and the longer she stayed, the more she risked. She risked being found out, and equally horrid, she risked falling more and more under Valin's spell.

Trying to forget her predicament, Emmie got up and retrieved the original Beaufort letters from the pocket in her petticoat, lighting a candle to examine them again.

She scowled at the words. "Here I am, here I remain. Thus one goes to the stars. Stop traveler. Three joined in one. Drat."

They had to mean something because the heading above them read "Monsieur d'Or's Exercises." Emmie kept staring at the words without much hope. They still seemed to refer to nothing she'd seen at Agincourt Hall, and it appeared she had wasted all that time spent cultivating Courtland and listening to his ramblings about the medieval history of the estate.

He'd spent a good half hour describing an old tower keep not far from the house. The young man had been so grateful for her interest he'd even shown her a drawing of the place, with its two towers joined from top to bottom by a massive internal crosswalk. She'd become increasingly confused once Courtland started talking about crenellations, forebuildings, and bridge pits. Old Henry Beaufort had refurbished Hartwell Keep upon succeeding to his title.

But as Emmie pondered this bit of information, she sat up from her slumped position at the writing desk in her sitting room. She picked up the phrase list and ran a finger down it.

"Tria juncta in uno," she whispered. "Three joined in one. That's Hartwell Keep! Two towers and the cross wall joined into one keep."

Bouncing out of her chair, Emmie strode up and down the sitting room while she thought. No wonder they'd been so unsuccessful. All the clues referred to the keep.

She'd go there tomorrow. Valin was taking the gentlemen to visit a neighbor's racing stable, the perfect opportunity. Emmie got back in bed slowly, for her chief dilemma remained. How was she going to feel about pilfering Valin's treasure?

She'd never stolen from someone for whom she cared. But Flash, Phoebe, and Sprout needed that gold more than Valin did.

She had to be strong. She had to resist the compulsion she felt in his presence. What did she think she could do, marry him? A marquess didn't marry a common thief, even if her mother had been a lady. And most men wouldn't want the illegitimate child of a governess, either. Except as a mistress, and Emmie had always resisted being made a pawn, a kept pet in the power of a man. She'd had enough being forced to endure a ruffian like Edmund Cheap; she wasn't going to put herself in an even more dishonorable situation. This she'd sworn to herself long ago. But then she hadn't imagined having to resist so beautiful a man as Valin North.

The next morning Lady Fitchett, Aunt Ottoline, and the other ladies embarked on a boating excursion on the ornamental lake in the park. After their visit to the racing stable the gentlemen were to join them for luncheon on the artificial island in the middle of the lake. Emmie pretended to have a headache until everyone was gone.

Obtaining a mare from the stables, she rode across the wood and out of the grounds maintained by the Agincourt estate. Half an hour's journey took her past the village that lay between the house and Hartwell Keep, which was situated on a hill that would have commanded a view of the countryside for the medieval lord of the tower.

She was still on North land, but the keep itself was uninhabited. Courtland was using most of his inherited money to restore it, but he'd run out at the moment and was waiting for the next payment from his trust. Thus there were no workers crawling on the scaffolding that had been erected against one of the towers.

Emmie rode up the hill and picked her way across the crumbling outer wall that surrounded Hartwell Keep. There was a makeshift wooden stair constructed against the base of the building. Emmie tethered her horse and climbed to the door, which was locked. This proved no barrier to Emmie's experienced fingers and slim metal tools.

Once inside she left the door open to admit light. Light also shone in from arrow slits and windows and from the gap where the roof once soared. Nevertheless, the building was so tall that light filtered in only so far, and she could only see dimly. She stood inside a vast hall. Courtland had told her he'd been able to restore the west tower, and Emmie was about to search for it when a shadow fell across the swath of sunlight from the door.

"Good morning, Emmie," said Valin.

Uttering a little gasp, she said, "Bloody damnation, you frightened me."

"Sorry." Valin came toward her, his boots sounding loud on the new floorboards, his features twisted into a thunderstorm expression.

Emmie watched him suspiciously. "What are you doing here? You went to the racing stable."

"I left early, and before you ask, yes, I followed you," he snapped.

Edging around him and heading for the door, Emmie shook her head. "I shan't remain here with you."

"Why not?"

"You know why."

"Ah, yes. There is that." His body tense with suppressed anger, Valin caught up with her and thrust out an arm to block her retreat. "You can go after you explain what you were doing prowling around my house in the middle of the night."

Emmie held her breath. After a moment's hesitation she turned slowly to face Valin, her mind racing. Had he seen her with the others in the Gallery Tower? Curse it. Now he knew she was looking for something.

Valin stood over her, his heavy-lidded eyes glittering even in the subdued light. "I saw you return to your room."

"To my room," Emmie parroted. Then he

hadn't seen where she'd come from. "Um, I couldn't sleep, so I took a walk."

"A walk. Rubbish, Emmie dear," Valin snarled, grabbing Emmie by the arms. "There are only a few reasons ladies go abroad so late—a fire, sickness, or to meet a lover. There was no fire, and you look damned healthy to me." Valin dragged her so close she could feel the barely restrained tension in his body. "So, my dear, *whom did you meet?*"

Emmie twisted out of his grasp and lifted her chin. "Don't be ridiculous, my lord."

"Aha! You did meet someone."

"Nonsense," Emmie said. "I met no one."

"Then what were you doing wandering around my house?" Valin snapped. "I know you met someone because you came from the direction of the Gallery Tower, and between your rooms and the tower lie those of the gentlemen and my apartments, so—" Valin stopped. His brows drew together as he glared at her. Then the turbulence of his expression vanished, and in its place came a look of astonishment.

"By God, you were looking for me."

Emmie gawked at him while her cheeks turned pink as she realized what he meant. "Um."

"Look at you. You're as red as a camellia." He paused, his brow furrowing. "Or am I imposing my own desires upon the case?"

"Well . . ." Stunned and trapped, Emmie took

refuge in attack. "Who are you to question me? What were you doing spying on me, lurking outside my bedroom?"

Valin pursed his lips and said nothing.

Emmie swallowed and whispered, "Oh. I didn't—that is, I hadn't realized . . ."

She jumped as Valin swore under his breath, took her hand, and kissed it. "Don't say anything. Come with me."

Astonished and confused, she allowed him to lead her up a tower stair to the third-floor landing. She balked when he opened a door and tried to usher her inside.

"No."

Valin cocked his head to the side. "I only want to show you something. I call it Courtland's folly."

"You won't try to—to—you'll be a gentleman?"

"I'm always a gentleman, Emmie."

"Humph."

She walked into the room and stopped to stare at the largest bed she'd ever seen. "Gracious mercy."

Valin joined her and together they contemplated the bed. The enormous four-poster loomed in the middle of the chamber, its columns more like architecture than furniture. They began as rectangular bases, surmounted by four small columns supporting a miniature roof. On the roof rested a giant vase, the top of which merged into the larger column that supported the carved canopy.

The whole wooden structure was of rich dark oak with gilded decoration, and had a headboard so ornate that it could have served as a paneled wall in an Elizabethan nobleman's house. A new brocade bedspread finished the impression of overdone luxury. Its decoration wasn't what robbed Emmie of speech, however. What was most unusual about the bed was its size.

Still gawking at the four-poster, she asked, "How many do you think it would hold?"

"Courtland says ten or twelve."

"Surely not twelve," Emmie said.

"People were smaller back then."

"Oh."

"They slept together to keep warm."

"Oh."

They stared at the bed some more. Then they gave each other a sideways glance.

Feeling awkward, Emmie looked away. "I suppose it was cold, what with no coal to heat houses." She was babbling and couldn't stop herself. "Sleeping all bunched up together would have kept the chill away. A good idea, really, all those people keeping warm in there, but it's terrible when families are too poor to afford more than one room and can't get away from the cold, with no big bed—" Valin's fingers skittering up her arm robbed her of speech.

"Are you cold?"

"Me? Cold?" Her mind went blank as she felt Valin's arm around her and she felt his lips on her cheek. Then he blew in her ear, causing a shiver.

"See," he said. "You are cold."

"I'm not, and you know it."

She felt his lips at the corner of her mouth even as his hand traced down her ribcage. His lips fastened over hers, his tongue darting into her mouth. Emmie knew she should push him away, but she didn't want to. She wanted to touch him, to know what his bare skin felt like. This urge won over all her mother's warnings about ruthless gentlemen. Funny how she'd never been tempted before, but with Valin, her body overruled notions of virtue—or survival.

Thrusting her hands inside Valin's waistcoat, Emmie kneaded his flesh, feeling the warmth of his body through the shirt. Suddenly that shirt was her enemy, a rude interference between her hands and what they wished to explore. She heard fabric tear, but dismissed the sound in her excitement. Acres of smooth flesh stretched tightly over lean muscle. Emmie pressed her cheek against Valin's bare chest and allowed her hands to follow the curve of his back, then drift lower.

She heard Valin catch his breath and felt his

hands move over her as hers were moving over him. In moments she felt her clothing drop from her body. A tiny voice shouted a warning, but the rest of her didn't care. She wanted Valin North, and she was going to have him—here, in this tower, away from the grime and ugliness of St. Giles.

As if to prove her own determination, Emmie began pulling at Valin's coat. He gave her a startled look, but didn't protest when she stripped him of his waistcoat and shirt. That was as far as she got before he lifted her in his arms and set her on the edge of the giant bed. As he followed her down into the covers, his lips touched her breast. Emmie clenched her teeth at the jolt of desire that followed.

Trembling hands delved into hidden places. Their kissing became more and more frenzied. Emmie clutched at Valin, digging her nails into his flesh as he touched her. Then he entered her, and she gasped, tearing her lips free of his and ducking her head into the hollow of his neck and shoulder. Valin whispered her name urgently, then began to move while distracting her with his hands.

In an unfamiliar country, Emmie wavered between pleasure and pain, but with Valin's expertise, pleasure finally won. She climbed a mountain of sensation, reached the top, and plunged hard. At the same time Valin cried out and joined her. They collapsed among the tousled covers, and Valin pulled her into the hollow formed by the curve of his body.

Although the physical eruption was over, Emmie felt as if her world and her body were still shaking. Already the chilly light of reason was invading the dark warmth. What had she done? She'd succumbed to this man whom she could never have. Hell to pay, that's what there'd be. Hell to pay. Just then Valin turned onto his stomach, and the sheet slipped off his hip. Her gaze slid over the curve of his buttocks, and Emmie smiled.

He was worth it.

12

❧❧❧

Drowsy and satiated, Valin opened his eyes as Emmie turned on her side away from him. Her breathing slowed, and he closed his eyes while his fingers played with a long auburn curl that fell down her back. He submerged himself into a world of sunlit warmth he knew wouldn't last, not the way he needed Emmie. Then his eyes flew open again.

What have I done?

Reason finally escaped the morass of cravings in which it had been imprisoned. He'd bedded this young woman, this adventuress. Would she expect marriage? Wasn't that why she'd come?

Think, North, old man. You followed her. She wasn't expecting you, and she tried to leave when she saw you. You were the one who sought her. You know you've wanted her all along. That's why you went to her rooms last night.

Very well, he thought, best be honest; he'd gone to her rooms to do what he'd just done. Only she hadn't been there, and he'd nearly howled with rage once he suspected she was meeting someone else. Then today when he realized she'd been looking for him—that they'd been looking for each other, he had been at once relieved, astonished, and triumphant. Part of him said, *Yes, this is what I need.*

He'd never understood what the word revelation meant until then. The shock of it had created a dizzy euphoria. The idea of showing Emmie Courtland's folly hadn't been a deliberate ploy. Perhaps he'd expected to share amusement with her, to prolong their moment together, but the sight of that ludicrous bed had been like a dry wind whipping across a grass fire.

As before, Emmie had ignited with him. She had stoked the furnace of their passion, her reluctance seared to ashes. Her response told him more of her need for him than any words.

And when they'd made love he'd discovered something else—she'd never been with another man. This lady adventuress with the secret past and lurid vocabulary was an innocent. He had assumed her experienced. Valin's fist closed around the curl he'd been playing with.

Dear God, he'd just made love to a virgin!

He sat up, staring at nothing, his jaw slightly adrift. Emmie had never been with a man. Holy hell. What did that signify about her feelings for him? *Dear God.* He hadn't expected this twist of circumstance. He wasn't prepared, not prepared at all. Emmie stirred and turned on her back. He glanced at her body, felt his own respond, and scrambled out of the bed.

"Valin, what's wrong?"

"Nothing, nothing, nothing," he said as he snatched up his trousers and wrestled into them.

His hands were shaking as he dressed, making him even more anxious to escape the allure of her presence. In a few moments his determination would crumble and he'd hurl himself on top of her again.

"Where are you going?" she asked. This time her voice had an edge to it.

"Forgot an appointment. Estate manager, accounts, legal matters, boring business. You know." He fumbled with the buttons on his shirt. Half of them were missing. He gave up and threw on his coat. "Have to go. I'm late. Sorry."

Emmie drew the sheets up to her chin. "You certainly are."

"What?"

"Don't forget your waistcoat." She pointed at

the foot of the bed where the garment lay twisted in the bedspread.

Valin grabbed it and retreated. "Sorry. The estate manager and my solicitor are waiting." He opened the door but made the mistake of looking back. She was sitting in the middle of that vast bed, green eyes wide, her hair wild, her shoulders bare above the sheet she clutched, the color gone from her cheeks.

"Forgive me, Emmie."

He stepped onto the landing and closed the door. Afraid to hear her calling him, he raced out of Hartwell Keep and rode back to the house at a gallop. He left his horse in the stables and was almost to his apartments, but suddenly stopped and retraced his steps. Moments later he was taking the Gallery Tower stairs two at a time. He reached Courtland's study only to find it empty. Rushing upstairs, he hurtled into a small library, slammed the door behind him, and fell against it.

Courtland glanced up from a book he was reading at a table. He saw Valin, and his mouth dropped open.

"I've ruined everything," Valin said. He groaned and lowered his head to his hands.

The younger man slapped his book closed and stood. "Damn, Valin, what's wrong? You look like you've been in a fight."

Answering with another groan, Valin stalked

over to a window where he proceeded to pound the stone embrasure. Courtland joined him, but Valin flung himself away and strode around the library picking up books and slamming them down, fiddling with pens and paper, glaring at a desk and an inkwell. Courtland watched him for a while, but only spoke when Valin subsided into a chair at the library table.

"If you're coherent now, how about telling me what's got you ranting like a Bedlamite. Has Acton done something terrible?"

Valin crossed his legs at the ankles and scowled at his boots. He was supposed to be the strong older brother, but he needed to talk to someone, and Courtland was a good listener, when he could be persuaded to turn his attention from his work.

"You must promise never to reveal what I'm going to tell you."

Courtland approached him, nodding. "Of course, old man."

Valin began with his discovery that Miss Emily de Winter was an imposter.

"And just now—" The words clogged his throat, and Valin clenched his jaw. "Let's just say I've committed myself irrevocably to Emmie."

"But you said—"

"I know what I said!" Valin paused and cleared his throat. "I mean that I've committed myself in a way that does not admit going back."

"Unless you signed some kind of agreement," Courtland began.

Valin growled, "I said irrevocable."

His brother met his gaze, and comprehension dawned. "I see."

"And I never intended to marry her. At least, well, I didn't think about it."

"Are you sure, Valin? I've never seen you so baffled by a woman, and I know I've never heard you talk about one more. You've been quite the old Valin lately."

"What do you mean?"

"You've been like you were before the fire." Courtland hesitated, then spoke gently. "You used to smile, old man. After the fire, the only smiles I saw were counterfeit. You know, the kind one uses in polite society. But now the real ones are back."

"Just because she may have done something to restore my temperament doesn't mean I should marry her."

"And you're not buried in work all the time."

"I don't work all the time."

"You do," Courtland said. "Even your forays into Society are work. For you. But since Miss de Winter arrived, you've actually enjoyed yourself. I think matching wits with her has changed you, old fellow."

Valin looked away. "There are some things that can't be changed, no matter how I wish I could."

"That's what's wrong!"

Eyeing his brother, Valin lifted his brows.

"You're afraid of what will happen if she hears those absurd old rumors."

They'd never talked about the fire so openly. Courtland had been a boy when it happened, and Valin hadn't wanted to burden him with the truth. But somehow he'd learned it anyway. Valin smiled faintly at his brother.

"You really believe those rumors are absurd?"

"Of course," Courtland replied.

Valin refrained from protest. The urge to unburden himself was almost irresistible, but his confusion about Emmie overshadowed everything.

"There's something else," he said quietly. "In an—an agitated moment, I called her 'love,' and she must have taken it literally, otherwise she never would have . . ."

Courtland was gaping at him. "You said that?"

"Only once. Don't leer at me, damn you. This whole situation is infernally confusing."

"Why?"

Valin threw up his hands and uttered a wordless sound of exasperation. They fell silent for a moment as Valin tried to make sense of his chaotic feelings.

"Courtland," he whispered. "I don't even know who she is."

His brother knelt beside him and placed a hand

on his arm. "Don't you think that's what has broken through that barricade of fury you've set up against the world?"

Valin gawked at his little brother.

"Come on, old fellow. We live in a tiny, inbred little world, a few hundred families at most. And Miss Emily de Winter descends upon you with her exotic manner of dressing and speaking, and then you find out she's an adventuress, that you don't know who she is. You're fascinated with this lady scoundrel not because she's a lady, but because she isn't."

"A damned stupid whim upon which to base a marriage!"

Courtland rose and walked back to the library table where he picked up the book he'd been reading. "You're shouting, old boy."

"How is that relevant?" Valin demanded.

"You might as well accustom yourself to the idea," Courtland said as if Valin hadn't spoken. "She's in your blood. You might say you're infected with her."

Valin bolted out of his chair. "Oh, what do you know of it? You spend your days with your nose buried in achievements and restoring old bed— er—in restoring old keeps." He pointed at his younger brother, who had started to grin at him. "What are you smirking at?"

"You. You're a bear with its leg in a trap."

Drawing himself up into a stiff posture, Valin looked down his nose at Courtland. "One would think you'd try to help me escape this predicament, or at least offer sympathy."

Courtland's book dropped to the table as he uttered a loud guffaw. He hurried around the table when Valin cursed and stalked out of the room. He caught up with Valin on the landing and clapped his brother on the shoulders.

"Sorry, old fellow." Courtland was trying to stifle a grin. "I do sympathize with your plight. Perhaps it would help if you actually knew to whom you've promised your hand in marriage." Unable to hold off his mirth, Courtland fell against the wall laughing.

"Cheeky sod," Valin muttered. He glared at Courtland, then grew thoughtful.

"But perhaps you've hit upon the solution after all."

⁂

Struggling into the skirt of her riding habit, Emmie kicked her corset aside. She'd been unable to tie it without help. Her tears obscured the garment as she began to cry again.

"Oh, bloody damnation." She knelt on the floor and picked up the corset, using it as a handkerchief. "Stop it, Emily Fox. Crying is useless and weak."

She stood, still wiping her cheeks with the end of the corset. Her gaze fell on the bed, the sheets, the drops of blood. Moaning, Emmie turned her back on the evidence of her folly and sat down on the clothes chest beside the window.

A life spent in the rookeries meant that she'd become familiar with the details of intimacy in a way no lady ever would. In fact, she'd been thirteen when a well-meaning dollymop from Whitechapel had revealed the mystery. But knowing and experiencing were not the same. Experience had been far more gratifying. Until Valin had bolted as if fleeing the plague, the sneaking varmint. She dropped the corset beside the chest.

How could he be so amazingly beguiling, so seductive one moment and so anxious to vanish the next? He was sorry he'd done it. That was why. He regretted making love to her even though he'd found it as amazing as she had.

Why had she abandoned all principle, all her carefully guarded honor? She had been content to remain untouched and alone before Valin North. Indeed, she'd been too busy providing for her siblings, her band of nefarious friends, and herself to worry about the absence of love in her life. Before she'd come upon the marquess, romance had been some vague notion encountered in the books

Mama had given her. Characters in a Shake-
spearean play involved themselves in romance, not
young women from the rookeries who were of
illegitimate birth. In any case, one couldn't count
on men. She was disgusted with herself for succumbing to one. Look what it got her—left alone
in the middle of a big ugly bed.

"Serves you right for trusting a man," she muttered to herself.

Leaning back, she rested against the stone wall
and closed her eyes. She wanted to run away, to
escape this boiling cauldron of unfamiliar emotions—longing, humiliation, pain—all mixed together.

Longing, humiliation, pain. And love. Understanding broke over her, an icy downpour on a hot
summer day. Love was the only explanation for her
mad conduct. Suspended in the midst of a swarm
of emotions, Emmie faced the truth. A hidden,
needy part of her had latched upon Valin's careless
reference to love, trusted in it, and fed its own
longing.

"Well, there it is," she whispered. "You're a
gullible fool in love with a man who's run away
from you."

Anguish overwhelmed her. She wanted to hide.
She wanted to curl up in some dark place far away
and whimper.

More tears slid down her cheeks. Emmie wiped

them with her hands as she sat up and straightened her spine. She couldn't run away, no matter how miserable she felt. She couldn't abandon her best chance of securing a proper future for her little ones. Besides, if she left Valin would alert the authorities. She'd have to go into hiding. If she did that she couldn't support herself for long without delving into the funds she'd saved for Flash and the others. That she would not do.

Scooping up the corset, Emmie rose and placed it on the chest. Her mouth set in a line as thin as a hatpin, she went to the bed and stripped the bottom sheet from it. After restoring the covers to their former neat condition, she folded the stained sheet and stuck it in one of the voluminous hidden pockets in her petticoat. She'd get Betsy to burn it. The corset vanished into another pocket.

A glance around the room showed her she hadn't forgotten anything. Emmie picked up her riding hat, stuffed it on her head. She'd stay even though she'd made the same stupid mistake her mother had made, falling in love with a ruthless nobleman.

"The sooner you find the gold, the sooner you can get away from him."

She had to stop tormenting herself wondering why Valin had bolted, why he suddenly regretted their lovemaking. Sighing, Emmie admitted to herself for the first time that she knew why. He didn't want to become involved with a lady adventuress. Emmie didn't blame him. What well-bred man wanted someone like her for a wife? Before Valin, she'd been resigned to this fact. Before Valin. Her thoughts were circling around the same miseries.

"Don't," she muttered. "Don't think about it. Get on with searching for the blasted gold."

Leaving the chamber with the giant bed, trying to ignore the pain in her heart, Emmie proceeded to explore Hartwell Keep. She had brought a copy of the foreign phrases with her. It was concealed in her hatband. Emmie removed the paper and read it again.

The Latin phrase "Three joined in one," the last on the list, must refer to the keep, and she had decided that the others must have been intended to be read in reverse order. The third phrase was a command, "Stop, traveler," which obviously was meant to warn the reader to remain at the keep when searching for the gold. The second, "Thus one goes to the stars," had to mean that she must go to the top of the keep. The gold must be hidden somewhere on the top floor of one of the towers. The first phrase, "Here I am, here I remain," could refer to the actual hiding place of the gold. Emmie mounted the tower stairs that led past the chamber she and Valin had been in and climbed to the top floor.

Over two hours' search of both towers and the
arcades that connected them proved fruitless. Emmie searched both towers a second time from cellar
to roof. No gold.

A black gloom settled over her, due more to her
having nothing to distract her from the loss of Valin than to not finding the gold. Weary in spirit
and body, Emmie left the roof of the west tower
and descended the winding stairs. She braced one
hand on the wall as she negotiated the twisting,
worn steps. From the top of the stairs all she could
see was a dark turn.

"Pestilential tower," she grumbled. "Why did
they have to make the bloody stairs wind around
like a corkscrew, damned twisted . . ." Emmie
stopped and contemplated the next turn.
"Damned winding . . . spiral!"

She hurried down the rest of the stairs to the
ground floor where she inspected the outside turn
of the stair. The flight was a curve of stone that
formed a little alcove.

"Under the spiral. Goodness gracious mercy."

Tapping her foot on the flagstones, she continued. "But not here. In Agincourt Hall. It was
there all along. Henry Beaufort, you were a clever
old devil after all."

Feeling her spirits lift a trifle, Emmie left Hartwell Keep and was soon riding out of the wood on
the Agincourt grounds. She walked her horse

across the Palladian bridge that spanned the ornamental lake. Voices carried across the water to her. On the artificial island, with its little Greek temple and wispy trees scattered across a grass-covered landscape, she could see the other guests.

The ladies' skirts billowed in the breeze, soft muslin and organdy with yards of lace and delicate straw bonnets tied with taffeta bows. The olive green, brown, and black of the gentlemen's frock coats contrasted with the pastels worn by the ladies. She could hear the clink of sterling silver on china and see black-clad servants moving among the diners. A gentleman bowed to a lady and offered a crystal wineglass. Two women with lacy parasols strolled by the water's edge. A maid offered a pristine white napkin to a lady in a gown of pale blue with white ribbons.

Emmie dismounted, entranced by the elegance and peace of the scene. Then, without warning, she began to feel separated from it in a way that had nothing to do with distance. She could never belong to that setting, really become one of those tranquil and refined ladies. Muslin, organdy, chivalrous gentlemen, pristine white napkins, and china—these didn't belong to her world. Valin knew that.

"And he couldn't tell me," she whispered to the mare standing quietly beside her. "Perhaps that's why he left."

Feeling aged and hopeless, Emmie mounted again and rode to the stables. Once she entered Agincourt Hall she forced herself to think of her search for the gold. She would test her explanation of the foreign phrases at once, in the Gallery Tower. It was the one in which Beaufort had put the chimneypiece. She still thought it was the mostly likely choice for a hiding place. But first she must bathe and change.

An hour later, Emmie had burned the blood-spattered sheet in her rooms. After fending off Betsy's prying questions, she set out for the Gallery Tower. On the way her thoughts turned to Valin. The gloom that resulted caused her to take a wrong turn, and she ended up in one of the rooms designed by Robert Adam. Frescoes of garlands and classical urns, columns and pilasters in white plaster greeted Emmie. It was the Blue Room, so called because the walls had been painted pale blue to contrast with the white of Adam's designs.

Emmie had taken only one step into the Blue Room when she noticed Lord Acton bending over a table. His back was to her as he picked up an octagonal inkwell and slipped it in his pocket. Emmie knew the inkwell was valuable because Aunt Ottoline had told her it once belonged to Louis XIV. Of red jasper with gilt trim and a gold fleur-de-lis set on top as a handle, it was a noticeable piece that Emmie would never have filched. She would have left then, but Lord Acton turned and saw her.

"Ah, Miss de Winter. Have you been standing there long?"

"I just came in."

"Good, good." Acton rubbed his hands together and smiled at her. "I'd like to have a little talk with you, if you could spare me a few minutes."

Emmie nodded warily. During their short acquaintance she'd developed a distaste for Acton. He was lazy, and considered the luxuries his position in Society brought him insufficient for the honor he did the world by his mere presence in it. He had Valin's gray eyes, without the light of intelligence that enlivened his brother's, and his hair was warm blond like his mother's. Although his build was as hard and muscled as a blacksmith's, Emmie was sure he'd run to corpulence in a few years, for Acton drank too much, ate too much, and smoked cigars whenever he couldn't indulge in the other two vices.

"Won't you sit down, Miss de Winter?"

Emmie took the chair Acton offered, her skirts spreading so wide they hid most of it. Acton seated himself beside her.

"Ordinarily I wouldn't embark upon such a conversation with a lady, but since you've become engaged to my brother in so surprising a manner, I feel I must."

"Indeed."

Acton glanced at the open door and lowered his voice. "I feel it my Christian duty to tell you something I know my brother won't. It's about the death of our father and stepmother."

"That happened long ago," Emmie said. "How can it signify today?"

With many expressions of regret at having to reveal such ugly truths, Acton poured forth a venomous account of the events at the old lodge.

"So you see," Acton said with an expression of grief and regret, "I had to warn you. Everyone is certain Valin tried to seduce my stepmother. Father interrupted them, and in the ensuing fight . . ."

Emmie toyed with the lace on the undersleeve of her bodice. "So what you're saying is that a boy of—seventeen, was it?—managed to overpower a man in his prime and a woman as well."

"Perhaps." Acton sighed dramatically. "Whatever the details, it's evident that Valin went there with dishonorable intentions and thus was the cause of both the quarrel and the fire."

Smoothing the yards of violet fabric that composed her skirt, Emmie rose and walked to the desk where the inkwell had been.

"How out of character for him."

"I beg your pardon?" Acton said.

Emmie glanced over her shoulder at him. "Your brother hardly lacks for feminine admiration. I find it hard to imagine him forced to go to such trouble to get it."

"You didn't know my stepmother, Miss de Winter. She was quite exquisite. And you're familiar with Valin's angry temperament."

There was a pen in a gilt stand in the shape of a shell. Emmie toyed with it while she considered Acton's words, wondering if he had been about to pocket it, as well.

"You're right. Valin does have an angry temperament."

Acton's eyes filled with satisfaction.

"However, he's also kind, honorable, and loving, and all of these far outweigh any ill temper he might display on occasion."

"On occasion?"

"In fact, my lord, the only person I've met in your family capable of destructive conduct is you. Good day."

Sailing out of the room, Emmie found a staircase and hurried down it.

"Sodding bloody smasher," she hissed. "Lying snoozer. Giving me that lay. No wonder Valin's in a temper all the time, putting up with the likes of Master Acton. Wish I'd of had a cosh. Knocked him a good one right on his head, I would."

Still muttering to herself, Emmie grabbed handfuls of skirt and trudged through a series of rooms on her way to the Gallery Tower. She couldn't very well explore if Courtland was around. The young man traveled up and down the length of the tower in search of books and artifacts he'd stored all over the structure. If he was still there she'd have to come back tonight.

Emmie crossed the vast expanse of the salon, which overlooked the terraced gardens and ornamental lake. She put her hand on the gold knob of a door that led to one of the drawing rooms. As the door opened she heard Valin and stopped. She couldn't bear to meet him. Not now.

In the middle of closing the door, she heard her name. Edging closer, she peeped into the room. Valin was standing beside a table bearing a crystal brandy decanter. Courtland poured a drink and shoved it into his brother's hand.

"Look here, old fellow. Be reasonable."

Valin gulped down the brandy and scowled at Courtland. "Reasonable? You're the one who followed me in here and started arguing. You don't understand. She's just not an agreeable acquaintance. She fell among bad companions. You should hear her language."

"Not like the precious dull ladies we usually meet, eh?"

Suddenly Valin threw his glass at the fireplace

where it smashed against the marble. "Damn it! You're altogether deceived if you think this is amusing. I told you. I don't even know who she is."

Courtland was silent for a moment. Then he said, "So how do you intend to get out of it?"

Emmie shut the door and stared at it unseeing. They weren't saying anything she hadn't already thought herself. But hearing it from Valin—only then had she realized how she'd secretly expected him to change his mind. Secretly she'd thought him great of heart, unlimited in understanding. Yes, she'd fallen in bad company. Had her companions tainted her?

Fighting tears, Emmie swore under her breath and hurled herself away from the drawing room door. "He's a hypocritical, poor-spirited creature. Looking down that aristocratic nose at fine fellows like Turnip and sweet girls like Betsy and Dolly."

Emmie wiped her wet cheeks and scurried across the salon. Her heart hurt again with a fine-edged pain she feared would never leave her. She had to find privacy in her room before she started bawling. The gold could wait. It had been there for hundreds of years. A few more hours wouldn't matter.

She'd find it and scarper as soon as she could. She didn't owe Valin North a thing. Taking his gold would be her revenge. A pity he'd never know about it. Of course, there was a consolation. When she hooked it, everyone in Society would think she'd run away from him.

He'd be humiliated. Yes, humiliated like she'd been at Hartwell Keep. In the years to come, she could think of that whenever she was fool enough to wish he'd really loved her.

13

"Ow!" Emmie turned and hissed into the darkness. "You stepped on my heel, Betsy."

"It's monstrous dark in here. Curse it, Pilfer, you're treading on my gown."

"Missus has got the lamp, and I can't see," grumbled Pilfer.

Emmie walked out of the topmost room in the Gallery Tower with Betsy and Pilfer behind her. Despite the risk, she'd been forced to bring a lamp in order to search the stairs. She'd left Turnip on the ground floor to stand guard while she and the others began looking.

"If the gold's at the bottom, why start at the top?" Betsy whispered.

"No sense searching all around unless this is the right tower. Hold the lamp."

Emmie knelt on the landing and began to examine the stone floor. "Bring the light closer. I can't see."

Pilfer hunted along the walls for a few moments, then stood behind Emmie. He clasped his hands behind his back and rocked on his heels.

"Whatcha lookin' for?"

"I told you," Emmie said, "Foreign words."

"Like carving?"

"Yes."

"I can read, you know. I can read twelve letters."

"I know, Pilfer, now be quiet."

She crawled toward the door that led to the room, her fingers brushing the stone. She couldn't see any trace of carving.

"I bet this one's an S."

Emmie's hands stilled and she looked over her shoulder. Pilfer's small finger was pointing at something near the first step of the spiral staircase. Scrambling around, Emmie crawled over to him while Betsy brought the lamp.

Faintly etched words appeared in the pool of light. Pilfer brushed away sand and dust to reveal the rest of the letters. The carving was worn and shallow and in an archaic script.

"That's it!" Emmie shoved Pilfer. "Why didn't you say so at once?"

"You said to be quiet. You weren't paying attention. You never pay attention to me. I told you I could read."

"Yes, yes. I'm sorry."

"So what's it say?" Betsy asked.

"*Sic itur ad astra*. Thus one goes to the stars."

"I know what that means," Pilfer said. "It means the stairs."

"'Course you know," Betsy muttered. "Emmie told us."

Emmie patted the boy's head. "That's very good, Pilfer. You've been a great help, so now we know we've got the right tower."

"See?" Pilfer sniffed at Betsy, who rolled her eyes and followed Emmie down the winding stair.

Their progress was slow. They had to make sure they didn't miss another phrase carved in the stone, but Emmie was almost certain that the next clue would be found at the bottom, under the spiral. Upon reaching the ground floor they met Turnip, and searched the area under the bend in the stairs.

However, try as they might, not even Pilfer could discern any carving. Emmie widened the area of the search to no avail. Soon she, Pilfer, and Betsy returned to the bend in the staircase to stare glumly at the flagstones. Grumbling, Pilfer kicked the ancient stone wall.

Emmie sighed. "Pilfer, don't do that. You'll damage the finish."

"Already crumbling, an' if I had a glim I could see where I was going."

"You can't have a candle," Betsy said. "We can't have wax dropped all over to show where we been."

Turning back to Pilfer, Emmie asked, "What do you mean, it's crumbling?"

"Got dents in it, has this rock."

"Where?"

"At the bottom here."

Emmie and Betsy gathered around the spot to which Pilfer pointed.

"Ha! It's not a dent. It's an *I*. There should have been an *S* in front of it, but the carving has been damaged. Pilfer, you're marvelous clever you are."

"I am?"

"Yes." Emmie pointed to the faintly carved letters. "It should read *'Si ste viator,'* or 'Stop traveler.'" She glanced from Pilfer to Betsy. "This is it."

Standing in a half circle around the carving, they looked at it for a while, then backed away from it slowly. Betsy held the lantern close to the floor. They bent low, except for Pilfer, and examined the flagstone in front of the carving. It was larger than most and a bit more regular in shape, almost square. Emmie stepped on it, tapped it with the heel of her boot, and exchanged triumphant glances with Betsy.

Everyone dropped to the floor around the stone, and with Turnip's help and the aid of a couple of crowbars, they were able to move it. A little shoving revealed a sliver of blackness beneath the flagstone. Emmie wiggled her fingers into the space.

"Right," she said. "There's a hole. Old Beaufort put it where people seldom walk."

Everyone stood by while Turnip wrestled the stone aside. Then Emmie took the lantern and held it over the blackness to reveal a dust-covered wooden stair, rickety and steep.

"Turnip, you stay here. No one's been down there in centuries by the look of it, so we won't be meeting unwanted company."

Holding the lantern in front of her so that light played on the top stair, Emmie tested each step as she went.

"Be careful," she said to Betsy and Pilfer. "The wood is thick, but it's really old."

They reached the base of the stairs without mishap, and Emmie held the light aloft to reveal a room carved out of bedrock. To her disappointment it was filled with ancient litter. Connected by open arches, two smaller chambers flanked the larger.

"That's what he meant," Emmie said to herself.

"What?" Betsy asked.

Emmie indicated the three rooms. "Three joined in one."

"Where's the gold?" Pilfer asked as he picked up an old chisel from the floor. "Coo, what's all this?"

Emmie glanced at the debris that formed an irregular pile covering a good deal of the main chamber floor. "Ancient rubbish, I suppose. Look for another carving."

This time their search proved fruitless. Emmie, Pilfer, and Betsy gathered at the rubbish heap and surveyed it.

"Nothing for it but to move this lot," Betsy said.

Emmie went to the stairs and whispered up to Turnip. "Everything quiet up there?"

"Fine, Missus."

Betsy and Pilfer righted a Tudor oak buffet that had been tossed on top of the heap, and Emmie set the lamp on it. Then they attacked the rubbish. They picked through an odd assortment—pikes, a bread paddle, medieval quarrymen's wedges, earthenware jugs and dishes, broken lances and scythes.

"Gracious mercy," Emmie said as she moved a disintegrating stack of baskets to reveal an iron cage used to hang torture victims from battlements. "Someone threw anything they could get their hands on in here."

Betsy straightened up with a brass hunting horn in one hand and a shield in the other. "I'm coming to bits of rock."

"That's not rock. That's parts of statues. Probably from the garden."

Beside her Emmie heard Pilfer catch his breath.

"Coo! Look at these." In his hand lay blackened arrow points, which quickly vanished into his pocket.

"What are you planning to do with those?" Emmie demanded.

"Nuthin'."

"Precisely, young man, because as soon as we get home you're moving in with Flash and Sprout and Phoebe, and you're going to school."

Pilfer let out a howl, and Emmie clamped her hand over his mouth while he danced in agitation.

"Quiet," Betsy said as she brandished a pitted sword.

Bending down to eye level with Pilfer, Emmie whispered, "You want to get lagged?"

Pilfer shook his head violently.

"Then look sharp."

She released the boy, and he went back to work with an aggrieved air. Emmie picked up a scarred chessboard along with a mason's level and a copper vat and stepped back. Her foot landed on something pointed, and she slipped. Her load of rubbish flew out of her hands. The vat landed with a bang onto something made of stone and spun to a standstill while the level and chessboard crashed behind her.

Emmie hopped on one foot, cursing the spiked mace head she'd stepped on, then stood still. Everyone listened. At last Emmie ventured a loud whisper.

"Turnip?"

The coachman's head appeared through the hole at the top of the stairs. "No harm, missus."

The three treasure hunters sighed in unison and went back to work. In a few minutes they had cleared the area of everything except an oddly shaped stone slab. Emmie grabbed the lamp, and they walked around the object, which was rectangular, except for a rounded end, and rather narrow. She stopped at the square end with Betsy to her right side and Pilfer to her left.

"Cor," said Betsy.

"Coo!"

"Goodness gracious mercy."

Pilfer made as if to touch the block with the tip of his boot but drew his foot back. Betsy pressed her skirts against her legs so that they didn't brush the stone. The lamp wavered in Emmie's hand. She glanced at Betsy.

"It's a headstone."

"Off a grave."

"Coo!"

They were silent again.

"There's a corpse under it," Pilfer said, and he backed away.

Emmie ignored him and set the lantern on the headstone. She brushed the surface with her hands, clearing away wood chips, mortar, and dust.

"I don't think there's anyone under it," she said. "See what's carved here? It's French and it says 'Here I am, here I remain.'"

Emmie, Betsy, and Pilfer exchanged grins. Then they shoved the headstone aside to reveal an iron ring set in another flagstone. A bit of struggling moved this last obstacle. Peering into the cavity thus exposed, Emmie beheld two caskets sitting side by side covered in dust. A few minutes work had them out of their hiding place. Betsy brushed them off with her petticoat while Pilfer produced a hammer and chisel. One casket was larger than the other, a plain chest of brassbound wood with a heavy lock. The other was a piece of decorative art, a jewel casket with curved sides and ornate gilded decoration.

Her tongue caught between her teeth, Emmie placed the chisel on the lock of the larger chest and aimed the hammer. As she drew it back for a strike, she heard something from the floor above. She recognized the sounds of a scuffle and blows. Then Turnip hurtled headlong down the stairs and collapsed.

Betsy cried out and rushed to him. Emmie dropped the chisel and ran forward as someone took the steps two at a time. She stopped short when Valin North stepped into the lamplight holding a pistol.

About his lips played one of his infrequent smiles. It was one she'd never seen—contemptuous, glacial yet malevolent—a smile one encountered on dark nights in Whitechapel alleys. Emmie's skin crawled as Valin walked over to her.

" 'Lay not up for yourselves treasures upon earth, where moth and rust doth corrupt, and where thieves break through and steal.' " Valin glanced at the two caskets, then back at Emmie. "I always believed the Beaufort treasure a myth, but I was wrong." His voice softened even as rage sparked in his eyes. "And you've been after it all along."

No one moved or breathed.

"By God, I've been a fool."

Emmie shook her head. "It's not like—"

"Shut up, Emmie, and open the boxes."

"But I—"

The pistol swung to point at Betsy. "Don't make me any angrier than I am already. I'd like to shoot you, but I'm sure wounding your little helper here would hurt you far worse."

Emmie bit her lower lip and watched him. His expression had a light, amused quality she didn't like. She had no notion what he might be capable of in such a mood. Without further protests she jammed the chisel into the lock of the chest and bashed it. The old metal snapped. Then she applied a hairpin to the jewel casket's delicate lock and stood back.

"Open it," Valin snapped.

Betsy brought the lamp, and Emmie lifted the heavy lid of the chest. It was filled with gold and silver. Valin glanced at the coins, at Emmie, and back at the coins.

"Those are Spanish," he said.

Emmie nodded. "Escudos and reals, I think." She picked up an irregularly shaped silver real. At the top was a crown above a large heraldic crest. The inscription read, *"Philippus D G Hispaniarum et."* She turned the coin over to see the remainder of the inscription. *"Indiarum Rex."*

"The Armada hoard," Valin said softly. "Open the other one."

Emmie tipped back the lid. She nearly gasped as the lamplight caught the gleam of gold and gems. She saw rubies, emeralds, and pearls.

"Jewels," she whispered. "I didn't know he hid jewels, too."

"So Henry Beaufort had a treasure of his own, not just the Spanish one," Valin said. He narrowed his eyes. "Those are sovereigns. That figure on them is Elizabeth I."

"And the reverse is a Tudor rose," Emmie said.

Valin eased closer to the glittering hoard and buried his hand in it. Cascades of precious metal and gems streamed through his fingers as he lifted a handful.

"My congratulations, Miss de Winter. You've found old Beaufort's hidden treasure when everyone else thought it was either a myth or lost forever." Valin tossed a coin in the air and caught it, keeping the pistol trained on Betsy the whole time. "Tell me. How did you find out about the story of the Spanish gold? You can hardly have heard it circulating in the slums of London."

He meant the question as an insult, the sneaking varmint. Emmie raised her chin and looked down her nose at him.

"I scarfed one of your Holbeins and found the riddles Beaufort left as clues to the location."

"You did what?"

Emmie smirked and planted her hands on her hips, imitating a superiority she hardly felt. "I plucked one of your prize paintings from under your very nose, my lord high-and-mighty. Not so clever as you think, are you?"

"I'm the one with the gun."

"You're not going to shoot Betsy or me or anyone."

"You're right," Valin said. The nose of the gun

dipped, and Valin started walking toward her. "But lying little lady thieves must take the consequences of their crimes. Want to know what the consequences will be for you, my dear?"

Emmie backed away and raised the hammer she still held. "Keep away from me."

"You led me a pretty dance, and it's time to take your punishment."

Emmie lifted her skirts and turned to run, but Valin snatched a fistful of fabric. Emmie stepped on a broken lance and slipped. Her skirt tore, and Valin laughed. He reached down and grabbed Emmie's wrist, but as he pulled her to him, Pilfer rushed out of the shadows and kicked him on the shin.

"Bloody mutcher! You leave the missus be."

Emmie yanked her wrist free in time to see Betsy rush at Valin with the bread paddle. Valin recovered in time to dodge the paddle and catch Pilfer by the back of his collar. Lifting the child, he let the lad kick his feet in the air and swear at him.

Valin rounded on Emmie while she was getting to her feet and pointed the gun at Betsy again. "Call them off."

She hadn't survived in the rookeries without knowing whether a man was capable of shooting women and children.

Edging away from Valin, she shook her head.

"You're not going to hurt Pilfer, and you're not going to fire that gun."

"But I'll fire mine, Miss de Winter. I promise you that."

Acton North stood on the stairs holding a revolver. It was pointed at Emmie's heart.

14

Megan the collie poked her nose through the hole in the floor and pricked her ears at the barrage of noise coming from the people in the room below. One of the women shrieked at Acton. Megan started and scrambled away from the hole. She circled it before settling down under the bend in the spiral staircase to wait for her master.

The din coming from the subterranean room rose higher. Betsy was giving Acton a frank appraisal of his character and appearance. Turnip held his sore head and moaned while Emmie snapped out her opinion of people who threw other people down steep flights of stairs and brothers who helped them.

While the verbal battle raged, Valin remained silent. Part of him wished he'd never gone to Emmie's room tonight, but he'd wanted to explain why he had left her at Hartwell Keep. Truthfully, he had also just plain wanted her.

By the time he'd reached her chambers, his decision had been made—he wanted to marry her, no matter what the consequences. A mad decision considering how little he knew of her, but what else could he do when life held no attraction without her?

When he found Emmie missing from her room yet again, of course he had looked for her—searched with a brain-fevered anger that stemmed from jealousy. Illogical as it had been, he'd made the mistake a second time of suspecting that she'd gone to some gentleman's room. Perhaps if he hadn't found it so hard to believe she cared for him, he wouldn't have flown across the house looking behind curtains, peering in alcoves, and listening at doors. His ear had been pressed against the portal of one of the gentlemen's guest rooms when he'd heard a distant crash.

Speeding downstairs to the Gallery Tower, Valin had spotted Emmie's coachman lurking by the spiral stair. Only then had he realized that Emmie and her little band were up to some kind of mischief, most likely robbery. At least he hadn't been fool enough to approach without first retrieving a gun.

By the time he'd gotten back with a pistol he'd had time to absorb the significance of what he'd seen. Emmie, or whatever her name was, had been lying to him even after he'd discovered her ruse. Since then—even at Hartwell Keep—she'd been weaving a fluffy warm snood of distraction around him. Her goal had been to keep him preoccupied until she could get to whatever was in that hole beneath the Gallery Tower. She must have wanted it badly to forfeit her honor. Had she always intended to make that sacrifice? Was he the first merely by coincidence?

At this thought Valin's frigid rage warmed in a furnace of pain. Everything he'd assumed about Emmie, about her affection for him, had been based on lies. Fury, humiliation, and agony threatened to wring a cry from his throat. When he had confronted her here in the darkness, she'd turned on him with frightening ruthlessness, with hatred. Valin swallowed and opened his eyes. He hadn't realized they were closed. Why was everyone yelling?

Betsy hissed at Acton, who was standing halfway up the stairs. "Listen, you sodding muck snipe. You speak to Emmie with respect or you'll see the sharp end o' my chiv."

"You make one move and I'll use this," Acton said, waving his revolver.

"Now, Betsy, hold your tongue, girl," Turnip said as Emmie helped him stand.

Valin was about to demand silence when the

child called Pilfer scampered up the stairs and kicked Acton on the shin. Acton yelped and took a swipe at the child with the revolver. Emmie dove for the boy and yanked him out of harm's way. Betsy squawked, grabbed an earthenware jug, and threw it at Acton. As it crashed on the wall behind its target everyone started shouting again.

Drawing in his breath, Valin put the full force of his lungs behind his shout. "Silence!"

He gestured with the pistol. "You thieves, over there away from the stairs."

Emmie held Pilfer's hand and marched over to stand with Turnip and Betsy. All four of them glared at him in defiance. He scowled back at the coachman, at the maid, even at Pilfer, but he ignored Emmie.

Acton came down to join him. "Excellent. I'll summon a constable, and he can throw them in jail while we—"

"Bloody macer," Pilfer said. "Missus, he's going to make lags of us all."

Another shouting match ensued while Valin subsided in confusion. He hadn't thought beyond surprising Emmie in the midst of her betrayal. Acton wanted to call the authorities, expose her to the world, send her to prison. Part of him, the raging deceived madman, wanted that too. But if she went to prison he couldn't see her pay for turning him into a fawning puppy; he couldn't force her to beg his forgiveness. God, he wanted to make her feel as stupid and ashamed as he did at this moment.

"Shut up, all of you!" Acton rounded on Valin. "Watch them while I send a servant to the village." He started up the stairs, tossing a jibe over his shoulder. "It will be gratifying to see this lot in Newgate."

Emmie and her little band went silent.

Valin blinked and said, "Newgate?"

Acton was almost up the stairs when Valin reacted.

"No."

Coming back a few steps, Acton said, "I beg your pardon?"

"We're not sending for a constable."

"Are you mad?" Acton pointed at Emmie. "That woman tried to rob you. She's an imposter, a thief, and no doubt a whore."

Valin turned slowly to his brother and said, "Use that word in connection with her again, sir, and I'll give you the beating I should have years ago."

"You're still besotted," Acton said. "Lord, Valin, after what she's done she deserves anything that happens to her. Don't let her make a fool of you again."

"I've no intention of playing the fool, Acton. I

simply want a more personal justice than our authorities provide. Besides, how do you think we'll appear once this little masquerade is exposed? The scandal will give Aunt Ottoline a brain fever from which she'll never recover. The rest of the family will never forgive us."

"But she tried to steal a fortune from us."

Valin was trying to remain calm, but his pain and rage threatened to erupt at any moment. Emmie's presence was a goad. She was standing in the dim light wearing a shabby black gown that only served to highlight her appeal, which in turn made him even angrier. He darted a glance at her and found her glaring at him with scorn. How dare she scowl at him as if he were the traitor? He was the injured one. Had she ever behaved honestly toward him, or had it all been a ruse? Of course it had. Her damned thieves' cant was more important to her than he was.

"Valin," Acton said. "What are you going to do?"

"Damnation!" Valin paced back and forth, then stopped near the stairs. "For now we'll lock them in their rooms. I have to think of some way to avoid scandal for Aunt's sake."

"Why don't you marry her?" Action sneered. "Then she can't steal from you."

Valin glanced at him. "You're such an ass. I'm going to see to it that she never steals from anyone again, but first Miss de Winter will break our engagement."

"She'll run away."

"She won't get a chance."

"And after the engagement is broken she can vanish. We can send her to the London authorities. No one will connect a common thief with your fiancée if we're discreet."

Valin threw up his hands in exasperation. "You have a devious mind, Acton. I congratulate you. Now will you please stop arguing and help me?"

"Very well."

Once the decision was made Valin finally felt a measure of calm. Perhaps he was dazed from the shock of Emmie's perfidiousness.

"Thank you, Acton. Then will you please take Miss de Winter to her room?" Valin retrieved a key from his waistcoat pocket and handed it to his brother. "Lock her in."

Acton motioned for Emmie to walk ahead of him. As she passed him Valin felt the small breeze created by the sweep of her skirts and smelled honeysuckle. Schooling his feature to impassivity, he looked at her at last. She sailed by him without a glance, and his last view of her was of those drab skirts floating up the stairs and vanishing above his head.

Late the next morning Valin unlocked Emmie's door and strode into the sitting room. She was dressed and standing at a window. She faced him as he approached, and Betsy came in from the bedroom.

"Ooo," Betsy said. "It's his high-and-mightiness."

Emmie gave her friend a bitter smile. "Don't be frightened, Betsy. He scowls like a bear with an ague, but he doesn't bite."

"If you're finished babbling, I've something to say to you."

"Chosen a jail for me, have you?" Emmie asked with a sneer.

"Lady Fitchett has found herself called away to London. She left early this morning."

"Cor, got rid of her, he did," Betsy said.

Valin gave her an indifferent glance. "You should be grateful I've kept up appearances by allowing you to attend your mistress." He turned to Emmie. "Pack your things. Be ready in an hour."

He took great satisfaction in leaving without further explanation. Emmie would stew and worry, thinking he'd decided to haul them to the village and hand them over to the constable as Acton had urged. His pleasure didn't last long, because it was derived from an act of small-minded pettiness of the kind he detested.

Thus his mood was foul when he went down

the front steps to find Emmie's coach waiting, with Emmie and her little band of thieves in their usual places. Acton was already mounted, his revolver stuffed unobtrusively in his waistband. Turnip slouched on the coach box eyeing the gun, but he made no threatening moves.

Emmie stuck her head out the carriage door. "Where are we going?"

Mounting his horse, Valin ignored her and pulled up beside Turnip. "Follow me, and don't do anything stupid. My brother will be beside you all the way."

They were almost at their destination when Emmie stuck her head out again and shouted at him.

"You sneaking nobbler, you can't throw us in there!"

Riding up to the forebuilding of Hartwell Keep, Valin wore a bitter smile. It didn't take long for him to supervise Turnip in moving Emmie's luggage into her new room. When Valin returned to the carriage, he ordered the thief to resume his post, then yanked the door open and stuck his head inside.

"Get out, Emmie."

She gave him a look he'd seen on Russian cavalry officers charging his troops in the Crimea and stayed where she was.

"If I have to carry you, it will be over my shoulder."

Emmie's gaze assessed his determination. She sighed and nudged her friend.

"Come along, Betsy. Pilfer, take care when you jump down."

"They're not coming," Valin said.

A chorus of protest ensued. He lifted a brow and brushed his coat aside to reveal his pistol. The volume of the complaints lowered to a continuous, fulminating grumble.

Emmie put her foot on the carriage step and scowled at him. "Where are you taking them?"

"Somewhere where they can't make mischief for me or help you."

Valin offered his hand. Emmie slapped it aside and jumped to the ground.

"I give you notice," she said as she lifted her skirts and climbed the stairs of the forebuilding. "You harm them, and I'll do for you, I will."

"It's quite amusing how quickly you lose your polished accent and cultivated expressions when you're frightened."

Emmie rounded on him, looking down from three steps above. "I ain't frightened, I'm furious at meself for allowing a false, mean, odious villain like you to—"

"To what?"

"Never you mind! I curse the evil wind that

blowed you in my direction, I do. And if it's cultivated expression you want, how's this one: 'The
villainy you teach me, I will execute; and it shall
go hard but I will better the instruction.' "

"I'm not the one who's the villain here."

With a sniff, she whirled around and marched
inside the keep. When he guided her to her new
room, she halted on the threshold. He watched her
eyes widen and her cheeks lose their color. Then
she walked into the room and continued past the
giant bed to stand looking out the window. Valin
waited for her to say something, to protest, but she
remained silent until he was about to close the
door and lock her in.

"You really are a bloody bastard, you know."

She didn't turn around, and he closed the door
softly and turned the key in the lock. He stared at
the thick wooden panels of the door, her words
echoing in his memory. He detested Emmie more
than he ever had Carolina, the only other woman
to provoke such a strong emotion from him. He
was going to figure out a way to prevent her from
working her evil on more unsuspecting gentlemen.

Back at the carriage Acton was waiting for him.

"Valin, this is absurd."

"What?"

"Allowing these criminals to go free."

"For the last time, Acton, I won't have them
prosecuted. It would be disastrous for Aunt Ot-

toline if it were known that she entertained a professional thief, even accepted her as my future wife. We're taking them to the village. Mr. Leslie is meeting us there with a couple of men who will escort our guests to the nearest port."

"I cannot believe you're going to pay for their passage to France," Acton said with a roll of his eyes.

"It will take them some time to get back, since I'm paying only for one-way passage. Please, Acton, no more discussion."

"Very well, but you're too soft."

In the village Valin's arrangements went without a hindrance, and two hours after leaving he was back at Hartwell Keep. Acton had gone home to keep Aunt Ottoline company. As he climbed the stairs to Emmie's new jail cell, he reflected upon how cooperative and sympathetic Acton had been. His brother had been greatly offended by the deceit practiced on Valin and conscious of the mortification and hurt that had resulted. Indeed, Acton was behaving very unlike himself. Perhaps all that had been lacking was some great crisis to bring forth his good qualities. Valin was grateful, for he'd never been so confused or felt so alone.

At this thought gloom descended upon him, a mood darker than the winding stairwell he was climbing. Valin reached Emmie's room, unlocked it, and gave the door a slight shove. It swung open noiselessly to reveal an unexpected sight. Emmie was standing in a pool of fabric; the yards of her silk skirt formed waves of indigo on the floorboards. The bodice of the gown and a corset lay on the bed.

She hadn't seen or heard him, or she wouldn't have continued to remove her delicate chemise. Valin stood in the middle of the doorway, his mouth slightly open in surprise, as Emmie pulled the chemise over her head. Watching her was torture—seeing the pale curves of her hips and breasts. His whole being suffused with his physical reaction to her. It was like swallowing a magic potion that drained all the ugly emotions from him— even his rage—and left only desire.

He must have gasped, because Emmie suddenly looked up and cried out. She stooped, grabbed her skirt and petticoats and shielded herself.

"Rot your soul, Valin North! Get out of here."

"Don't screech at me. How was I to know you'd be—"

"Civilized people knock and ask, you bloody fool."

Valin's feet seemed to move of their own accord, and he found himself approaching Emmie as she backed away.

"I forgot," he said. He seemed unable to tear his gaze from her bare shoulders or exorcise the memory of her naked body.

Emmie kicked a length of midnight blue silk out of her way as she moved farther from him. "What kind of gentleman forgets the simplest of courtesies?"

"What kind of lady undresses in the middle of the day?" Only a minuscule portion of his mind heard what she said. The rest was on fire.

"A lady who's tired of waiting for her luncheon and wants a wash after a dusty trip, that's what kind." Emmie bumped into a dresser behind her and edged along it. "You stop where you are, Valin North."

Valin kept easing toward her and whispered, "Do you know you're the most beautiful thing I've ever seen?"

That stopped her. She fluttered her lashes, then said, "I am? But you've seen many women. I'm not as pretty as Miss Kingsley. I know I'm not."

"Miss Kingsley is irritating in her perfection. She's like a petit four—every tiny curlicue of her icing is molded into place. She hurts my eyes with her perfection." Valin stopped within touching distance but kept his arms at his sides. "You are real, Emmie. I love your nose, your fingertips, your toes, especially the little one that turns sideways. I love the way your ears turn pink when I kiss you. I love that little scar on your left wrist."

Emmie hugged her skirt. "I got it when I was a

girl, trying to filch lace at a shop. The shop owner chased me with some scissors."

Valin slowly lifted a hand and touched one of the curls on her shoulder. "I love the way your hair is always trying to escape those elegant arrangements you concoct for it." He bent and kissed the curl, then turned to find her staring at him, her face a few inches from his. "I love everything about your appearance, Emmie."

Dear God, he still cared for her. Deceitful and hard of heart as she was, he even loved her. He closed his eyes, willing himself not to feel what he knew he couldn't control, then he looked at Emmie, and lost his soul in her eyes.

"Oh, Emmie, I'm so sorry."

"Me, too."

Valin kissed her, his lips settling over hers as if they belonged nowhere else. He was already aflame, and when he slipped his arms around her, skirt and all, a wave of painful arousal swept through him. It made him desperate. He lifted Emmie and almost ran to the bed. A moment's feverish struggle with his clothing, and he sank inside her. He felt Emmie's nails sink into his buttocks as he moved, heard her gasps, and allowed the fire to engulf him.

15

❦

Emmie heard Valin cry out her name, but she was trapped in her own realm of wicked pleasure, too breathless to respond. When he fell to her side in a tangle of indigo skirts and his own clothing, she lay in the vastness of the bed trying to catch her breath. Her eyes flew open in surprise when Valin rolled on his side to face her with a bemused expression.

"I still have no notion who you are."

"Doesn't seem to matter a precious lot."

"No, it doesn't seem to," he replied with a grin.

She smiled back, but before she could say anything else, someone banged on the door. They both started.

Valin scrambled out of bed and ran to the door. "I didn't lock it!"

Emmie dove for her chemise while he spoke to someone on the landing and shut the door.

Emmie had turned her back to Valin so he could fasten her bodice. "Who was that?"

"A man I sent for. He served under me in the war, and I knew I could trust him to look after you."

She whipped around, dragging her loose skirts close to her body, and scowled at him.

"You mean you got me a jailer?"

"No, just someone to see you don't get into mischief."

"A sodding bloody nose to keep me in this salt-box!"

"This what?"

"This prison cell, you evil cur. You said you were sorry."

Valin furrowed his brow. "I meant I was sorry you were a thief and lied to me and that you—"

"Be quiet!" The blood drained from Emmie's face while she regarded Valin as she would a piece of rotten meat. She teetered on the brink of cataclysm as she realized her assumptions about their reconciliation were misguided. "You said you were sorry just to get me to bed."

Valin straightened his shoulders. "I would never do that."

"You just did, by heaven."

"You said you were sorry, too."

Emmie fastened the last button on her skirt, picked up Valin's boot, and threw it at him. Valin was trying to get the other one on his foot and hopped out of the way. The boot hit the door and slid to the floor.

"I meant I was sorry you deceived me, too," Emmie said, her temper hotter than a steam boiler. "Sorry you're such a coward you run at the thought of conceiving an attachment to the likes o' me. I'm sorry, I am. Sorry you made love to me when all the time you meant to keep me like an old lag. Pestilence and death to you, Valin North!"

She grabbed a candle in its stand from a nearby table and threw it at him. Valin ducked, and the missile hit the wall beside the door. Frustrated, breathing hard, Emmie's gaze darted around the room looking for a weapon. She flew to one of her trunks, found a pair of soft kid walking boots, and threw one at him. It hit him on the shoulder.

"I'll teach you to play such tricks on me."

She rushed at Valin, but he snatched his other boot and darted through the doorway. He slammed it just as she reached it. Emmie pounded on it and shouted at him.

"Sneaking bloody coward, you come back and face me."

Valin's voice came through the door. "Calm down, Emmie."

"I ain't no dollymop that you can—"

"No what?"

"No tart, you dullard." Emmie banged on the door. "Show yourself, you bloody, lying, sly, deceitful, sneaking . . ." Emmie ran out of breath.

"I'm sorry, Emmie. I'll come back when you've calmed a bit."

"I've had enough of your kind of sorry. Come back this moment so I can punch you," Emmie snapped.

She put her ear to the door, but that only blocked all sound. She stood back and kicked it, then yelped at the pain in her bare toes. Sinking to the floor, she wrapped a hand around her foot and cursed the day Valin had been born. She glowered at the remaining kid boot in her other hand. Tossing it aside, Emmie drew her knees to her chest, wrapped her arms around them, and lowered her head as tears came. She heard a door slam and the nickering of a horse, then the sound of Valin riding away.

Misery overwhelmed her. She'd allowed her desires to overrule her head again. Why had she been so foolish as to assume Valin regretted rejecting her? Because she'd wanted him to be as in love with her as she was with him, wanted it so badly she imagined sentiments that weren't there.

If only she hadn't been undressed when he entered the room. She had spent the time after he left looking for a way out. The last half hour passed with her hanging out the window in the hot sun searching for the best anchorage for a rope. What an evil chance that she'd decided to give herself a quick wash while she considered whether it would be best to escape by going down to the ground or up to the roof.

She was as weak as her mother had been. Emmie moaned and thrust herself up from the floor to pace in front of the bed. If her fortunes continued in this manner, she would end up with child. That meant disguising herself as a widow and moving to a decent part of London. She couldn't afford that along with her other expenses.

"A child!" Emmie sank to the end of the bed and stared into space.

After a few minutes she smiled slightly. A child of Valin's. Then her mouth settled into a tight line. What kind of life could she give a child? She would have to give up her only way of gaining a living in order to be a respectable mother. Then how would she provide for herself and her family?

"No," she muttered. "It won't happen."

If it did, she'd simply have to steal lots of valuable things before she gave birth.

Her hands were shaking. Emmie glared at them;

this was no time to lose control. She drew in a deep breath and let it out slowly.

"Keep busy."

Rising from the bed, she went to the trunk that held her hats, shoes, and jewelry. She opened it, then glanced over her shoulder at the door. Was anyone outside? Emmie thought a moment before dragging a bench across the room and leaning it against the door. She returned to the trunk and pulled out several drawers. Her hand fit inside one of them where she slid back a panel to expose a hidden compartment. Her fingers touched a latch, and the drawers swung aside to reveal her bag of tools. She opened it and checked the contents—a rope, a hook, the hammer and other implements she'd used in her search for the bloody treasure.

The rope might not reach the ground, but she couldn't test it. Someone might see it in daylight. If Valin took it from her—no, she wouldn't make that mistake. She had to get away from Valin before she was lost forever to her own weakness.

❧

After midnight, but before the moon set, Emmie was again hanging out the window. She had decided her rope wouldn't extend far enough for her to jump to the ground. She would have to attach the hook and throw it up to the roof. Luckily the keep had a crenelated battlement. All she had to do was toss the hook hard enough to reach a crenel. Once it caught, she would climb up and sneak down past the sleeping guard.

Emmie had been surprised that her jailer, whose name was Yarlet, was slumbering so deeply. He wasn't drunk, but he was on a pallet outside her door snoring so loudly he had startled the ravens that nested on the roof. However, she wasn't going to question this bit of good fortune.

Her petticoat was stuffed with items essential to her escape, including money she always kept in one of its pockets. She would remove the collapsible hoop, but without it her skirt would be too long. So she would tie it up, then replace the hoop when she got to Green Rising, the town with the nearest railroad depot.

Periodically she glanced at the surrounding countryside in case Valin decided to make another surprise visit. Once she had chosen the place at which to aim, Emmie ducked back inside. Luckily she happened to take a last look outside and saw a man riding up to the keep. Cursing, she pulled the wooden shutter closed and scurried about the room hiding the evidence of her activities.

She was sitting on the chest at the end of the bed when a key turned in the lock, and the door swung open without a sound. Emmie was taken aback to see Acton North slip into the room and close the door carefully. She rose, her arms folded, her expression cold.

"What are you doing here?" she whispered.

Acton spoke quietly as well. "I've been worried, so I came to see you."

"I steal things, but I'm not stupid. You're not worried about me."

"Of course not." Acton walked over to her, riding gloves in one hand, crop in the other. "I'm worried about Valin. He's more upset than I've ever seen him, and Aunt Ottoline has taken to her bed. She never takes to her bed, despite her never-ending complaints. This debacle has made her truly ill."

"I'm sorry, but Valin—"

Acton's voice rose. "I don't want to argue!" He bit his lip and glanced at the closed door. When Yarlet's snores continued, he went on. "Anyway, it's Valin I care about."

Emmie studied Acton's distracted manner with growing conviction. His hands wrung the gloves, and his eyes held pain and grief.

"I didn't want things to be this way," she said.

"I realize that now. I've been concerned with my own interests, but now I understand how badly Valin feels. He doesn't eat or rest. This is torment for him. So I think it's best if you leave. Now."

Giving Acton an evaluative stare, Emmie took a while to respond. "You're letting me go?"

"Yes. I've brought a spare horse. It's in the woods. And to make certain you stay gone, I brought the jewel casket. It's not the whole treasure, but it's enough to keep you in fine style for the rest of your life."

"Oh, certainly. It will keep me until Valin sets the police to hunting me."

Acton shook his head. "Don't concern yourself. He cares little about the treasure, and he won't go hunting for it or you. That would bring the notoriety Aunt Ottoline fears the most. He'll forget about you and the treasure rather than risk her health."

Emmie hesitated. Her life had been full of such choices. She was used to compromising her honor, her honesty, her character in order to survive. The treasure would secure the future for Flash, Phoebe, and Sprout. Much as she detested taking it from Valin, she couldn't afford such nice scruples. Scruples were for those who could feed their children and keep them from the slums of London.

In any case, Valin had already made his contempt for her quite plain. He desired her, but he also detested her, and she could no longer bear being near him knowing how he felt.

"Very well. Wait while I prepare."

With a sigh of relief Acton complied. Emmie packed a carpetbag, blessing her good fortune that she hadn't removed her crinoline before Acton appeared. She slipped into a cloak and bonnet and joined him. Acton opened the door. Motioning for her to follow, he led her past Yarlet, out of the keep, and into the woods. The mare she'd ridden at Agincourt Hall was waiting for her. Beaufort's casket was wrapped in canvas and placed in a saddlebag.

Acton held the reins while Emmie mounted, then handed her an envelope. "Here is a ticket. It's for the morning train to London. I'm sure you can handle yourself once you're there."

"Thank you." Emmie put the envelope in the pocket of her cloak.

"Don't thank me. I'm doing this for my brother."

"I know what it's like," she said softly, "doing things for other people."

"It's a new experience for me, but I find I quite like it. And by the way, Valin sent your friends across the Channel to France. You'll find them in Calais."

"I'll get them back. Farewell, Acton. I never thought you'd be the one to help me."

"Neither did I, Miss de Winter."

Kicking the mare into a trot, Emmie guided the horse to the path that would take them to Green Rising. If Acton watched them, she didn't know it, for she never glanced back at him or in the direction of Agincourt Hall and Valin North.

16

The morning after he made love to Emmie at Hartwell Keep, Valin sat in the small breakfast room trying to eat. If he looked at the ham, eggs, and muffins on the sideboard he grew nauseated, so he stared out the open French doors at the terraced gardens, the rolling green lawn, the ornamental lake. Next he attempted to drink the tea poured for him. His stomach didn't rebel, so he took another sip before thoughts of Emmie returned like midges, stinging him and provoking the anguish of spirit that threatened to become permanent.

He attempted another distraction by staring at a painting of the battle of Trafalgar over the sideboard. An odd choice for a room in which an appetite was a necessity. The artist had depicted ships aflame and watery explosions. Turning from the battle scene, Valin let his gaze fall on a framed drawing of Nonesuch Palace, then on a portrait of one of the Beauforts, a girl in the stiff damask gown, farthingale, and French headdress of the Tudor period. The square neck of the bodice, the undersleeves bursting with designs in gold thread, and the close-lipped expression all reminded him of the painting Emmie said she took from his London town house.

Emmie . . . He'd forced himself to stay away from her. She hadn't believed that their brief rapprochement had been based on a misunderstanding. She thought he'd deliberately tricked her into making love. Last night he hadn't slept for thinking of her, and in the long hours of darkness he'd finally realized something. He was trying to hold on to her, had been since he'd discovered her trying to rob him. Because even as he'd realized she was betraying him, the thought of her leaving him had been unbearable.

Unable to let Emmie go despite his pain, he'd grasped at any excuse to keep her. Something primitive had roused inside him and compelled him to make her stay—to hold on to her no matter the cost. All the other reasons—revenge, justice, his family's reputation, even poor Aunt Ottoline's health—paled beside this elemental need to keep and possess her.

Last night he finally admitted the futility of trying to make Emmie stay with him, to possess
someone who didn't want to be possessed. He of
all people should have known. Had he not rebelled
against such a possession years ago? And if she
knew the truth about him, she might recoil. He'd
rather face never seeing her again than watch her
dear little face when she found out he'd been responsible for such suffering. She may have her own
secrets, but they could be nothing compared to his.

Rising from the table Valin walked to the open
doors, stood in the breeze, and stared across the
landscape. The sun burned gently through a light
mist and turned dew on crimson rose petals to
silver. How could the world be so beautiful when
his mood was so ugly?

He must let Emmie go. With her she would
take the better part of his soul and all of his heart.
He didn't think he would survive.

How could he, when the person who made his
life complete was gone? Valin shook his head rue-
fully. Emmie was fascinating, even when she was
hurling verbal javelins at him as she had yesterday.

*I meant I was sorry you deceived me, too! Sorry
you're such a coward you run at the thought of conceiving
an attachment to the likes o' me.*

As the words ran through his head Valin gripped
the window frame until his knuckles went white.
"Bloody everlasting hell."

She'd been telling him all along, and he hadn't been listening. She'd wanted to tell him she was sorry for deceiving him. She had wanted to reconcile. Because she cared for him. But he hadn't listened, and he'd left her there rather than resolve their misunderstanding.

"Ass." Valin rested his head against the window as he lashed himself for the fool he was. His temper and his obtuseness had probably destroyed Emmie's affection for him.

Behind him, someone walked into the room. Valin glanced over his shoulder to see Acton stretching his arms and yawning.

"By Jove, I should have stayed in bed."

Without expression Valin returned to his study of the landscape. "You were out past two o'clock. I'm surprised you're up before luncheon."

"Is it that late?" Acton poured himself tea and sat down as a footman placed a loaded plate in front of him. He dismissed the footman.

"It's almost eleven." Valin's temper stirred. "You're up to your bad habits again."

"Not as bad as usual. I'm only half as hungover. I went to old Puffy Timson's card party."

"I told you not to—"

Acton raised a hand to ward Valin off. "Don't have a fit, old man. I won, and I only bet what I could afford this time because I'm tired of listening to your complaints." Lifting a fork in the air, he smiled. "I've decided the only way to avoid your scolding is to moderate my pleasures."

"Good."

"Besides, this debacle with Miss de Winter has me worried about you." Acton glanced at Valin's untouched plate. "You don't look well."

Courtland appeared in the doorway. "I agree. You look terrible, Valin. Any kippers left? I've been up since five trying to find references to old Beaufort's treasure in the family records."

"Never mind the treasure," Acton said. He rose, went to Valin, and placed a hand on his brother's arm. "See here, old man. You're losing weight. You're pale, and you're miserable. I was wrong about turning our little band of thieves over to the authorities, but you were wrong too. You should release Miss de Winter and send her away."

Courtland was piling kippers on a plate. "I agree, old fellow. I keep telling you it's mad to hold her prisoner. It's doing you more harm than it is her."

Valin nodded, deep in thought. "True."

"And she'll never tell you anything," Acton said.

Courtland sat down with his kippers. "Exactly."

Valin regarded the two solemnly.

"You must see it," Acton said in a quiet tone of certainty.

Walking over to Courtland, Valin slapped his

brother's back. "You're both right. I'll release her."

"I'll go with you," Acton said. "It's better if you don't see her alone."

Valin was already headed out the door. "I don't agree. For what I have in mind, seeing her alone is exactly the right thing."

It was almost noon when Valin arrived at Hartwell Keep. As he dismounted, Yarlet rode into view with a basket over his arm.

"Morning, lordship. I'm just back from the village with the lady's breakfast. She hadn't stirred when I left, but likely she's awake by now."

On the way upstairs Valin began to frown. What if he'd ruined everything with Emmie? She was convinced he'd deliberately tricked her into making love. She might hate him. She might not listen, the way he hadn't listened. If he couldn't resolve this misunderstanding, he'd have to let her go no matter what it cost him. His honor demanded it, dammit.

By the time they reached Emmie's door he was scowling, his disposition as foul as it had ever been. Yet he almost laughed at himself. Before Emmie had come into his life he would never have noticed the descent of gloom and ill temper. Because of her he was aware that his humor suited that of a demon with a toothache.

Yarlet knocked on the door and unlocked it. As the portal swung open Valin strode in quickly, determined to finish this business as soon as possible. He was halfway across the room before he realized it was empty. Looking around the room, Valin went cold. Emmie's luggage stood open, her gowns and possessions strewn about the room.

Valin stared mindlessly at the gown of indigo blue, but he snapped out of his daze and shouted, "Yarlet!"

The man stuck his head inside the room. "Lordship?"

"Miss de Winter is gone."

"But she was here," Yarlet said as he looked around the room in astonishment.

"When?" Valin went to the window and examined it. "When did you last see her?"

"Last night, lordship. I brung her supper and ate mine."

Growing colder, Valin left the window and approached Yarlet. "And after that?"

"Well, let me see." Yarlet rubbed his chin. "There weren't a sound out of her after I took her tray out. I had me own supper, and it was so quiet I fell asleep and didn't wake, 'til dawn. You said not to give her no trouble or disturb her 'less she asked for something, so I left her alone."

Valin said nothing, and Yarlet asked, "Shall we go after her, lordship?"

"What? Oh." Valin's gaze strayed back to the indigo gown, and pain stabbed through his chest. She had left him without a word. "No. There's no need." He closed his eyes against the images the indigo gown evoked. "I was going to release her, anyway, and she's been gone a long time."

Valin dismissed Yarlet and prowled the room, furious with himself for discovering the truth about his own and Emmie's feelings too late. He would find her. He had to.

He didn't know how long he roamed about that deserted room, but eventually he heard footsteps on the stairs. Acton shoved the door aside as he walked in with Courtland on his heels.

"I was worried."

"I wasn't," Courtland said, "but he wouldn't stay home so I came, too. I say, where is she?"

Valin picked up the indigo dress again, savoring the way it cascaded in soft folds from his hand. He breathed in the scent of honeysuckle. "She's gone."

Acton surveyed the room and shrugged. "She's a thief. We should have expected her to try to escape."

Valin returned to the window and looked down at the woods.

"Evidently she's an excellent thief, to have escaped this place," he said. Suddenly he frowned and leaned out the window, looking up at the roof. "An uncommon good thief indeed."

His brothers joined him.

"What are you looking at?" Acton asked.

Valin came back inside and straightened his coat. "How did she get out?"

"Through the door, I suppose."

Courtland shook his head. "It was locked."

"And there's no rope hanging from the window to the ground, or anywhere else," Valin said.

"Then she must have taken it with her," Acton said as he threw up his hands. "Really, Valin, what does it matter? She's saved us the trouble of releasing her. Forget it, and let's go home."

Courtland latched on to Valin's arm and began to lead him out of the room. "Yes, let's go home. I need to examine the caskets again so I can get a better idea of their age."

"Must you make even a treasure seem tedious?" Acton asked him. "We should be trying to cheer Valin up, not bothering with moldy caskets."

A mulish expression appeared on Courtland's face. "The coins and jewels are of historical importance."

The quarrel continued all the way back to Agincourt Hall, but Valin hardly heard it. The shock of finding Emmie gone was fading, and he was left in his own inner hell. The world seemed to re-

move itself to a distance. Even the horse underneath him seemed insubstantial compared to the
soul-destroying agony in which he lived. He'd
driven her away with his clumsiness, his foul temper, his lack of perception. This was the source of
his pain. This and the fact that there was no guar-
antee that he'd be able to find his bewitching, re-
bellious, and fascinating Emmie. If she could
discover a treasure no one else had found in hundreds of years, she could evade him forever.

And what if he did find her, but she wouldn't
listen to him? The uncertainty tortured him. Valin
vaguely realized his brothers were still arguing as
they reached Agincourt Hall. He trailed them upstairs. On the landing Courtland appeared in front
of him, which forced Valin to look up.

"Valin, old fellow, wake up."

"Yes?"

"The key. You locked the caskets in the Russian
room. Remember?"

"This is absurd," Acton said. "Valin doesn't
want to look at the damned treasure. Can't you see
he's upset? Let's find some brandy and have a
smoke."

"Artifacts relating to the Armada are of incom-
parable historical significance, Acton. I'm not
waiting." Courtland held out his hand to Valin.

Valin found the key in his pocket and gave it to
his brother. Following Courtland into the room,

he slouched into the nearest chair and lowered his head in his hands.

"They're gone!"

Lifting his head, Valin saw Courtland standing beside the table where they'd left the chest and jewel casket. It was bare. Valin rose and walked over to stare at the place where the treasure had been.

Acton laughed. "By Jove, she's made off with the loot, after all! What a woman."

"How could she have taken it?" Valin asked in a stunned voice.

"I don't know," Acton said, "but it's obvious she has, old man."

Courtland's eyes were wide. "Amazing."

Valin felt his black mood recede. He drummed his fingers on the table, thinking quickly.

"No," he said.

"What do you mean, no?" Courtland asked.

Valin crossed his arms over his chest and walked back and forth before the table. "There was no rope at the keep, and this room was locked when we got here."

"You're not making any sense," Courtland said.

"This whole thing has unhinged you a little, Valin," Acton said. "Forget about the treasure. You didn't want it. We don't need it, and you certainly don't want to report the theft."

Valin was still pacing. At this last comment he stopped in front of Acton.

"You're acting against your character of late, dear brother."

"Blast it," Acton said. "You've been chivying me about my conduct for years, and now that I'm trying to reform, you complain."

"But have you reformed?" Valin asked quietly.

Courtland went to Valin's side. "Now you're not making sense again."

Valin held Acton's gaze. "What doesn't make sense is Emmie getting out of Hartwell Keep without leaving any trace of her methods. What doesn't make sense is Emmie taking the risk of getting caught coming back here for the treasure, when she could get clean away. What doesn't make sense is how she could have vanished without a trace—unless she had help."

"Then Yarlet must have let her go," Acton said with a twisted smile.

"And then gone to fetch food for someone he knew wasn't there anymore?"

Courtland was frowning. "I say. That is odd."

"Emmie's gone, and the treasure's gone," Acton said.

"She wouldn't have had the time to get here on foot, steal the boxes and a horse, and get away before someone noticed." Valin moved closer to Acton. "Come to think of it, only a member of the family could take a horse without causing an uproar."

Acton pounded the table. "Damn you, Valin!"

"You were out late last night."

"I'm always out late."

"And you've been trying to prevent us from looking at the treasure ever since Courtland mentioned it."

"I was concerned for you."

"You helped Emmie get away, didn't you, Acton?" Valin walked around the table and approached his brother, who retreated.

"You're mad," Acton said.

Courtland looked from one brother to the other. "I say."

Valin stalked toward Acton. "You let her go, and that's why there's no rope at the window or sign of scratches on the door lock."

"She's a thief, for God's sake," Acton said as he backed away from Valin. "She escapes from places."

Valin backed Acton into a corner near a display table and grasped his lapel. "And the reason you let her go was so I'd blame her for the disappearance of the treasure instead of you. By God, Acton, I should thrash you bloody." He gripped Acton's shirt and dragged him close. "Tell me where she's gone, dear brother, or I'll make you wish you'd jumped from the roof of Hartwell Keep rather than lie to me."

Acton's mouth worked, but no sound came out. Valin smiled.

"And while we're having this little conversation, you're going to tell me what you said to convince her to go."

"I didn't—"

Valin looked over his shoulder. "Courtland, don't we still have an assortment of torture instruments?"

"In the armory," Courtland said with awe.

"Be a good lad and fetch a few of them for me."

Acton tried to jerk free of Valin's grip. "You aren't going to do anything to me."

Valin shoved his brother against the wall, and Acton's head knocked against the wood.

"To find Emmie, dear brother, I think I might break you on the rack."

17

Emmie stood in the children's playroom and watched Flash instruct Phoebe and Sprout in the game of chess. Flash's rules were original and tended to change with his moods, but that didn't seem to bother his siblings. She had spent three whole days visiting her little family, days that began early with a walk in Hyde Park and ended early with bedtime stories. Days full of ordinary activities, humble tasks, and peace.

During this visit she had enjoyed many things a lady shouldn't: mending, dusting and polishing furniture, preparing meals. Usually her days were filled with schemes, tricks, and scrapes with the law, and the regularity and peace of such ordinary tasks were a refuge. This was the kind of life she longed to lead permanently—not one of luxury, but one filled with tranquility and love. Emmie was quite certain she'd never be able to afford her dream.

Leaving the children to their game she went downstairs to the drawing room, found her bonnet, and put it on in front of a mirror in the hall. A pale little face looked back at her. It had been over a month since she had left Hartwell Keep and sent for Betsy and the others in Calais.

Her lack of color reflected the strain and wretchedness of those weeks. At first she'd hidden in the rookeries in case Valin came after her. Days passed, during which she alternately dreaded his finding her or hoped he would come. Then she would castigate herself for wanting him to appear and sweep her up in his arms. The past couple of months should have taught her she could depend upon no one but herself.

As the August days lengthened into weeks, desperation compelled her to set watchers to spy on the North town house. Always the report was the same. The place was deserted, and no one seemed to expect the marquess to come to London. She continued to have the place watched anyway. It wasn't until a few days ago that she'd been able to overcome her confusion and decide she needn't remain in concealment.

Tying her bonnet ribbons, Emmie slipped on her gloves and picked up a leather case by its handle. Inside, wrapped in velvet, were Henry Beaufort's coins and jewels. She hadn't gotten rid of them. Ordinarily she would do that as quickly as possible, but she delayed at first because she thought Valin would hunt her down through them. Later she decided the pieces were too distinctive to sell in England, and she should send them overseas. Once this decision was made, she still hesitated.

Betsy and Turnip grew annoyed with her reluctance to turn their find into money. A shouting match ensued, with Betsy accusing Emmie of not wanting to sell the treasure at all. After denying this vehemently, Emmie admitted the truth of the accusation to herself. She didn't want to sell the jewels and coins. Much as she hated to admit it, she thought of them as her only connection with Valin. Sometimes, though, she hated the sight of them, blaming the shining hoard for her misery.

If she hadn't discovered the clues to their hiding place, she would never have sought out Valin's company and been caught in a trap of her own design. She would never have fallen in love with the sneaking, lying varmint. And the longer she kept the treasure the more difficult it was for her to contemplate selling it. It wasn't hers; it was Valin's. She had never stolen from someone she loved.

"Goodness gracious mercy," Emmie said to

herself as she left the house. "What a time to acquire integrity."

She got into her carriage and leaned out the window. "To the bank, Turnip."

"Yes, missus."

Emmie settled back against the squabs and gazed out the window at the sunny streets. If she wasn't going to get rid of the treasure, she would put it in the bank. It was the safest place. Meanwhile she would compensate Becky and Turnip out of her own pocket.

That would be another strain on her purse. Her solicitor, who knew her in her guise as the children's lady guardian, had informed her that the time for paying Flash's school fees was approaching. She had but a couple of months. In addition, Phoebe would need a proper governess rather than a nurse. Soon she would be moving Pilfer into the household, and he would need special tutors to bring his education up to the standards required of Eton and Harrow.

Emmie began to feel overwhelmed again. Since she'd come home, her grief over Valin had served to make her other burdens more onerous. Sometimes it seemed all that kept her going was the knowledge that Flash and the others had no one else upon whom to depend.

The trip to the bank passed without incident, and Emmie returned to the boardinghouse. She washed, changed into her Mrs. Apple clothes, and was putting away the bank documents when Dolly appeared and danced across the room in excitement.

"Hello, luv!"

"What's gotten into you?" Emmie asked as she sat down at her desk.

Dolly pranced over to the desk and winked at her. "Heard a bit o' news at the Black Peacock last night."

Emmie's heart battered against her ribcage. "About the marquess?"

"Him, nah. What would I hear about him? I heard of a lady's maid what's down on her luck in the servants' lurk next door, so I went over and made her acquaintance, like. Her name is Kitty, and she told me her mistress tossed her out 'cause the master couldn't keep his hands to himself. Their name's Bagshot."

Dolly poked Emmie with her elbow. "Upstart folk they are. Come from a family of secondhand clothes sellers, but come into blunt selling sewing machines."

"So?"

"So Mrs. Bagshot has a mountain of jewels. Mr. Bagshot don't believe in safes and banks, and all them necklaces and things is just laying in a locked closet."

Dolly dropped to her knees and shoved Emmie's shoulder. "It's just the kind of lay you like. Old Bagshot and his missus is mean, sly creatures. They don't pay their servants hardly anything, and work them near to death. Tossed poor Kitty out without her wages, they did. Now she has no blunt and no character to show anyone who might hire her."

"She'll be on the streets in a week."

Dolly nodded. "Sooner."

Emmie traced the grain of the wood on the surface of her desk. If she managed this lay, she might be able to send Valin's treasure back and use the new haul to provide for the children.

Turning to Dolly, she said, "You and me, Dolly. No one else. We'll split everything equally."

"You're a good friend, seeing as how it's you who knows how to get into houses and locked places."

"You found Kitty and thought up the lay, so it's equal shares."

While Dolly chattered on about what she would do with her newfound wealth, Emmie's spirits rose. She might be able to send the treasure back to Valin! Guilt had been weighing on her like those enormous black iron anchors on the freighters at the docks. If she returned the jewels and coins, at least she could comfort herself with the knowledge that Valin could no longer accuse her of stealing from him. Perhaps his opinion of her would improve a little. Perhaps . . .

If only he'd been able to forget what she was and forgiven the lies she'd told him. But that was too much to ask of anyone, and he didn't know about the children. Before she could start crying, Emmie dragged her attention back to Dolly and listened to her plan a bright new future for them both. She smiled at her friend's enthusiasm, although she didn't share it. Without Valin, no future of hers would ever be anything but desolate.

❧

In a respectable if modest boardinghouse on the edge of the East End, Valin North prowled his rooms. He strode across the tiny sitting room to the bedroom and back, muttering to himself and occasionally glancing out the window at the traffic in the street several floors below. Rain had left the street wet, and the sweepers were busy clearing horse dung. He heard the cry of a flower vendor. A milk wagon passed by, then a chimney sweep with his load of brushes.

Having forced Acton to admit his involvement in Emmie's disappearance, Valin shook his brother until Acton's head nearly snapped off. That was enough to elicit the fact that Emmie had fled to London's East End. Valin had rushed to the city immediately and reengaged Mr. Mildmay. He, the inquiry agent, and his staff had been searching ever since.

After all these weeks, Valin was beginning to think he'd made a mistake in hiring the man. The world of rookeries, thieves' kitchens, and low taverns seemed impenetrable. Even the detective's contacts had never heard of Emmie.

His time in the East End had served as a lurid introduction into the world in which Emmie lived. He'd learned about the infamous Holy Land in St. Giles, the most notorious criminal slum in England, of Seven Dials, Jacob's Island, and Friar's Mount. This last was an open space in Bethnal Green, Spitalfields littered with putrefying animal corpses. He wouldn't have believed the place existed if he hadn't gone there himself.

Where was she? How did she live in this place? How had she remained as fine as she was, when her days were spent among people who robbed children of their boots, stole laundry hanging out to dry, and purloined packets of silk from milliners' shop girls? And these pursuits were some of the least nefarious of those he'd encountered. The whole of London from Blackfriars to the docks and beyond was a teeming infestation of human misery and degradation. Yet Emmie's spirit seemed untouched, a pure crystal among rubble.

He had to find her. He couldn't bear to think of her in this place. It was driving him mad.

Valin strode back into the sitting room and picked up a paper from the chair where he'd laid it. It was a drawing of Emmie. He'd made it himself from memory. He'd had it printed, and the package of copies had arrived. His men were to take the drawing with them and try to find someone who could identify it. Since no one seemed to know Emmie, he would find her by her face, her beloved face.

Valin smiled at the portrait. He hadn't quite captured her air of teasing confidence, but it would do. His men would go to boardinghouses, pubs, and street vendors until they found someone who could put a name to the picture and, with luck, an address.

God, the longer the search took, the more desperate and anxious he became. He wasn't even sure how to mend things once he found her. All he knew was that he had to get her out of this place permanently. He didn't want the damned jewel casket back; what he really wanted was to make her return with him to Agincourt Hall. Given her present opinion of him, she would refuse.

Valin scowled at Emmie's portrait. "You'll have to come back. I don't care what you want. This is no place for you. You're not staying here, even if I have to abduct you."

Sighing, Valin remembered how hard it was to keep Emmie if she didn't want to stay in a place. Yet here he was chasing after her like a demented hound.

"God help me," he said to Emmie's portrait, "I'm never going to stop loving you, even if I never see you again."

What if she wasn't in London? She could have left. Acton had said the East End was her destination, but that didn't mean she had remained here. At this moment she could be in another city, in another disguise, charming another man.

Valin dropped the portrait as he gazed at the building across the street without seeing it. He'd been so busy trying to solve the mystery of Emmie he'd never considered another man. Why not? Because he'd been the first man to touch her. But that didn't mean there wasn't another man. What if there had been someone else all along? No, there couldn't have been. He refused to consider the possibility.

While he was struggling with such thoughts, someone knocked. It was one of Mildmay's men come to report another unsuccessful search of the area of Shadwell. Another soon arrived with the same news for Seven Dials in the West End. Valin was discussing their strategy for using the portraits when Ronald Mildmay came in, his sorrowful expression in place.

"You haven't found her, either," Valin said as he closed the door behind the inquiry agent.

"Oh, yes, m'lord, I have."

The news was so unexpected that Valin didn't react for a few moments.

"Where!"

"It wasn't a question of where, my lord, but who."

"Mildmay, what are you nattering about?"

"We've been looking for the wrong person, my lord."

Valin scowled at the man. "We have not."

"I beg your pardon, but we have. The young person you know as Emmie is in reality someone called Mrs. Apple."

"Nonsense, man. Emmie has never been married."

"That's as may be, m'lord. Nevertheless, the person you seek goes by the name of Mrs. Apple. I have excellent information from a contact in Whitechapel who emerged from the rookeries only this morning. We're lucky he has been hiding from the police and needed money, or he'd never have talked to me about her."

"Why?"

"Honor among thieves, my lord. It seems Mrs. Apple is an accomplished leader of a gang of professional burglars and tricksters. She and her people can get into a place, strip it of valuables in minutes, and leave no trace."

"I could have told you that."

"Mrs. Apple isn't an ordinary thief, my lord. She's what's called a swell mobsman, one of the elite who preys on the wealthy. Not a picker of bank clerks' pockets."

"Where is she?"

"She lodges in Madame Rachel's Boarding House in Needle Street, off Blackfriars. Not the most improving residence, but certainly above the slum courts and ditches."

"Ditches?"

"Yes, my lord, a bedding place for many unfortunates, I'm afraid."

"Come, Mildmay. Take me there—no. No, if I'm going to succeed, I must know more." Valin beckoned to the inquiry agent, and they sat down in armchairs beside the tiny fireplace. "I want to find out everything about Mrs. Apple, Mildmay, and you're going to help me."

18

❦

Following someone without being detected and yet not losing them proved to be more difficult than Valin had expected. Dressed in shabby clothing obtained from a street vendor, he lurked for three days in an alley near Madame Rachel's in Needle Street, his legs and feet growing numb from standing in one place. His first sight of Emmie leaving the place had set his heart pounding and blood roaring through his veins. Then there had been no more time to be upset if he expected to keep up with her.

Emmie walked everywhere—to button and lace shops, to the chemist, to a blacksmith's, and to places the purpose of which seemed impossible to divine from their outward appearance. These premises boasted no signs declaring the business carried out within and no bay windows in which goods beckoned to customers. Valin dared not go inside for fear of running into Emmie. Three days of trailing along in her wake forced him to realize that she navigated the disreputable regions of St. Giles, Whitechapel, and Clerkenwell better than he did the rooms of Agincourt Hall.

By the fourth day, Valin had decided that following Emmie hadn't informed him as much as he'd hoped. He met Mildmay for dinner and remarked as much.

"You do realize, m'lord, that an evening watch might prove more interesting."

Valin crumbled a roll over his plate. "Damn. Why didn't you tell me before?"

"I was making inquiries as to the security of the neighborhood surrounding Madame Rachel's. If your lordship is determined to continue, such a nocturnal expedition should be safe as long as you're armed."

"I have my pistol, of course."

He returned to his post after dark and determined that Emmie was still in her rooms by the light in the corner window on the third floor. Around eleven o'clock the light in the window went out, but Emmie didn't leave the boarding-house. The hour passed slowly, and Valin had almost decided to go home. He moved nearer a street lamp and read his pocket watch. It was past midnight.

"You're being absurd," he muttered. "What can you hope to learn that you don't already know?"

Stuffing the watch in his waistcoat pocket, Valin was about to leave when two women came out of Madame Rachel's. One was much taller than the other. Veiled, mantelets on their shoulders, shrouded entirely in black, they were widows of little fortune.

Valin watched them come down the steps and set off in the direction of the train station. He turned up the collar of his jacket and grinned. Poor but respectable widows seldom strolled about London after midnight, but he knew a certain lady thief who would. Besides, the shorter one moved with Emmie's distinctive walk, like a small schooner on a glassy sea.

Stepping off the curb, Valin hurried after the women. He followed them onto a train that took them to the West End, past Westminster, along Hyde Park, and into Kensington. The farther west they went, the more deserted the streets became and the more uneasy Valin grew. They left the train at the edge of Kensington and walked to a group of new and expensive villas arranged around a square. Valin hid behind one of the brick pillars in a wrought iron fence and watched the widows slip around the side of the house and down the servants' stair.

"Good God, she's on one of her robberies."

He craned his neck to see where they'd gone, but the blackness at the bottom of the stairs had swallowed them. He crept down after them, only to find himself confronted by a locked door. Emmie and her companion had vanished. Valin peered in a window at more darkness and cursed himself for not anticipating this setback.

"Now what shall I do?"

He pulled his jacket tighter against the evening chill and trudged up to the street. The metropolitan police patrolled such areas as this regularly. Not wishing to be seen and questioned, Valin went into the garden that formed the center of the square and slouched against a tree.

Inside the Bagshot residence, Emmie knelt beside Dolly in a closet the size of her sitting room at Madame Rachel's. The Bagshots were at the opera, according to Dolly's information. Neither understood Italian or liked the music, but they went anyway, so that Society would see them. Meanwhile the servants had been given the night off so that Mr. Bagshot wouldn't have to pay their wages.

The only inhabitants of the house were a couple of maids who slept in the attic, and the butler.

Emmie turned a long, thin tool in the lock of a jewelry box. There was a click, and she lifted the lid. Dolly opened one of her petticoat pockets, and Emmie tipped the contents into it. They emptied three more boxes, more jewels than either of them had ever found in one house in London. While Emmie returned the jewelry boxes to their shelves, Dolly stood watch. She touched a heavy silk gown hanging in the closet.

"Grand clothes she has," Dolly whispered. "Too bad she looks like a gouty otter."

"Shh."

Emmie stood back and surveyed the closet in case they'd left anything out of place. Her gaze fell on a pair of men's boots. They were old and heavy, the kind farmers wore.

"What are these doing here?"

Dolly glanced at them and shrugged. "No accounting for the habits of them that's got lot's of blunt."

"But you can usually count on them getting rid of anything that reminds them of their humble background."

Emmie picked up one of the boots and turned it over. She heard a soft thud and shook the boot. Something fell out and rolled on the floor. Dolly picked it up, but it was too dark in the closet to see what the object was. They went to a window where Dolly held it up to the moonlight.

"Goodness gracious mercy," Emmie whispered reverently.

"My eyes," murmured Dolly.

In her hand rested a fat roll of one-hundred-pound notes. Emmie whipped back into the closet and dumped the other boot. Another roll fell out, and she tucked it into a petticoat pocket. She closed the closet door, and she and Dolly crept downstairs and out of the villa. As they walked down the street, Dolly hissed at her.

"Several thousand pounds at least!"

Emmie nodded and placed her hand on Dolly's arm to keep her from dancing down the street.

"Plus the jewels," Dolly continued in a low voice. "We're rich."

Too astonished to speak, Emmie nodded again. Who would have thought the Bagshots would keep that many valuables in a simple locked closet? She wanted to shout with elation and cry at the same time. If the jewels were real, the children's future was secure; yet no amount of money could make her future seem anything but bleak.

❧❧❧

Valin had resigned himself to a long wait, but less than an hour passed before the widows appeared out of the blackness and walked unhurriedly back the way they'd come. He should have realized Emmie wouldn't take longer than necessary to purloin whatever valuables she was after.

Following at a distance, Valin lost what was left of his patience. Emmie seemed calm and unconcerned that she'd just committed a crime, that she might be caught at any moment. The two women chatted as they walked, as if strolling at midday. Their unconcern only fed Valin's anger.

Emmie was mad, running about the city at night, without protection, breaking the law, exposing herself to the possibility of violence. He wouldn't allow it! Mrs. Apple was going to retire.

He decided to confront Emmie at Madame Rachel's. His immediate concern was that she not get caught with whatever she'd stolen. He was relieved when they made it onto the train without incident, but grew worried again as he thought of the trip back to the boardinghouse through so many disreputable streets.

Then the women gave him a jolt. One got off the train, and Valin nearly panicked. Both were still veiled, but he knew the one departing wasn't Emmie. He stayed on the train and left when Emmie did.

Now he grew more and more worried, for she was on foot and traveling deep into the squalid back quarters of the old city. The farther east they went, the older the regions became. Soon they passed areas where noxious slaughterhouses lay, and around such industrial regions clustered block after block after block of grimy, decayed tenements. In all his explorations of the East End, Valin had never come so far into the rookeries.

On and on Emmie walked—swiftly, with assurance and no hesitation. Fearful for her, Valin closed the distance between them. They traversed dozens of leaning tenements huddled around black, stinking waterways thick with sewage. The West End might be sleeping, but the East End had just gotten up. Valin could hear raucous laughter, and more than once he dodged insistent prostitutes.

He hurried after Emmie as she entered an area where old yards and gardens had been built over and landings occupied, so that the whole evolved into a maze of foul nests and burrows. Again he closed the distance between them and slipped his hand into the pocket where his gun was concealed.

Emmie startled him by ducking into a hole in a wall, but he went after her only to find himself in an open area formed by back-to-back cheap houses. She skirted a row of latrines and walked swiftly down a tiny passage to come out into a lane. To Valin's disgust a cess-trench had been gouged down the middle of it, leaving ledgelike paths on either side of the trench. Valin gagged at the stench and imitated Emmie by keeping to the narrow edges. Several dirty and drunken men huddled over a fire near a doorway, and watched Valin pass with slit-eyed curiosity.

Valin grew alarmed as he realized Emmie had paid them no attention. He decided to stop her and force her to leave this horrific place. He sped after her into an open court. Unsupervised children played amid water barrels, a pigsty, and more latrines. He dodged through another hole cut through a rickety tenement and stumbled over something. As he fell his head exploded in pain, and he heard a hoarse voice.

"Not 'ard enough. 'It 'im again."

Valin dropped to the ground and rolled. Something whizzed by the space where his head had been. As he jumped to his feet, a boot jammed into his stomach. Valin doubled over, then dropped to his knees under a blow to his shoulder.

Something clattered on the bricks beneath him. The pistol. He dodged sideways to avoid another blow. His vision was blurred, but he could see the two men wielding cudgels sidle toward him. He dared not take his eyes from them to look for the gun.

One more step and they'd be close enough for a strike. Valin braced himself as the two drew back their cudgels. Then he heard a noise behind him and turned in time to see two strangers clamber through the tunnellike passage into which Emmie had vanished.

Certain he was doomed, Valin backed away from them. They hardly glanced his way, brushing past him to plant themselves before his attackers. One was tall and thin as a ferret, while the other could have been a prizefighter. Valin's attackers straightened up at the sight of these two, but kept their weapons ready.

The ferretlike man spoke. "Evenin', Jakes, evenin', Toad. Missus Apple says to go about your business."

"That's what we're doing, like," replied Toad, whose extraordinarily wide mouth and jaw combined with a low forehead and pop eyes to make him worthy of his name.

"Right," said Jakes. "Missus Apple's got no call to interfere in our business, Snoozer."

Snoozer glanced at his companion.

"Pr'aps you've misunderstood."

"No, we ain't, Sweep," said Toad.

"Yes, you have," Sweep replied. "This here bloke is under Missus Apple's protection. I take that serious, I do. It's me job, and I always do me job. So if you don't rub along right quick, me and Snoozer is going to take offense, like." A knife appeared in Sweep's hand. "Hook it, you two."

Snoozer lumbered closer to Toad. "Yeah. You know what happens to old lags what trifles with

Missus Apple's friends. 'Member old Porkpie Leech? Lost half his skull and walks sideways to this day. And they never did find Snubbin Brown."

"Yes, they did," Sweep said. "Found 'im in an old latrine hole in Lurker's Alley."

"They did? When?" asked Snoozer, turning to his friend.

"The other day. Some tike was playing near it and saw these eyes staring up at 'im from the hole."

"Dead eyes?"

" 'Course they was dead. Who'd stay in a hole if they was alive?"

Valin listened in fascinated horror as the two conducted this conversation as if they were at a pub. Toad and Jakes, however, turned and ran. When Valin's new friends looked around they were gone.

Sweep removed his cap and scratched his head. "Missus was right. Toad'll believe anything."

"And Jakes won't stand up in a fair fight," Snoozer said.

"I beg your pardon," Valin said, "but I'd like to thank you for helping me out of a rather bad spot. Where is Emmie—Mrs. Apple?"

Snoozer regarded him solemnly. "Missus says we're to take you home."

"Good. I desire to have a word with her," Valin said.

"Nah," Sweep said as he put his knife away. "We're taking you to your place, toff."

"No," Valin said. "Take me to Mrs. Apple."

The knife reappeared, and Snoozer picked up Valin's gun.

"Pr'aps you need persuading, toff," Sweep said. "Missus don't want to see you. She says you should go back to the country and leave honest folk alone."

"Honest folk?"

The two drew closer, and Valin went cold as the gun's nose pointed at him.

"You look sharp, old lag. If missus says you're to go home, you're going home. If missus says you leave her alone, you do. Otherwise things could get a mite unpleasant."

Valin looked at one and then the other, noting the air of confident determination. He would have to cooperate for the moment.

Simulating outrage, Valin raised his voice. "Very well. If that's the way she wants things, I'll leave. You can tell her I don't care if she rots in this cursed place."

Unimpressed, Snoozer motioned toward the opening through which he'd come. "Just so's you go."

Valin turned on his heel and left. They stayed behind him all the way out of the slum courts. It took quite a while to get to an area where hansom cabs dared ply their trade, and when he reached a street where several sat, his escorts hailed one before he could.

To his chagrin, they remained with him on the trip to his boardinghouse. He could tell they were surprised at his destination, but he wasn't in the habit of explaining himself to thieves. He jumped down from the cab and slammed the door.

"Tell your mistress she can keep what she took from my house. I'll be gone from London in the morning."

"Whatever you say, toff."

He watched the cab drive away and hurried up to his rooms. He spent the rest of the night stewing and feeling like a fool, because it was obvious Emmie had spotted him and led him on a chase for her own amusement. The next morning he packed and left the boardinghouse. In case Emmie's minions were watching, he went to Paddington Station and boarded a train. He got off at the first stop and went back to take a room at his club.

Having rid himself of unwelcome observation, Valin spent the morning planning and making certain arrangements. Last night's excursion had turned into a nightmare. He could never have imagined a place so full of human degradation and misery, even after all he'd seen in the Crimea. There was comfort in the fact that he was doing his best to keep veterans and their families from descending to the kind of desperate poverty that festered here.

If only he could do more. He couldn't change it all, but he could change a small part of it, Emmie's part of it. Mrs. Apple might rule the rookeries, but he was going to see to it that she abdicated.

19

Emmie tapped her pen against the inkstand on her desk, noticed she was doing it, and stopped. "You're sure he hooked it back to the country?"

Snoozer rubbed his thick neck and nodded.

" 'Course we are. Seen him get on the train ourselves, di'n't we?"

"All right," Emmie said. She opened a drawer and handed each man a small envelope. "There's a little extra for all your help."

"Aw," Snoozer said. "It weren't nothing, missus. Not after all you done for us, paying our way out of jail afore we got the boat. I wouldn't a liked Australia."

Emmie smiled at them. She kept the smile plastered on her face until they were gone. Then she lowered her forehead to the desk. She hadn't thought it possible to be more unhappy than she already was, but last night proved her wrong.

She'd spotted Valin as she and Dolly left the Bagshot residence and nearly stumbled over her own feet in shock. It had taken great effort to pretend to be unaware of him and continue on her way. All the while Emmie's head buzzed and her heart pounded with elation.

He'd come for her after all!

A haze of euphoria had overwhelmed her satisfaction at the richness of the proceeds from the burglary. Valin must have forgiven her for deceiving him and found that he loved her anyway. Why else would he go to such great trouble and spend untold amounts of money to find her?

She'd expected him to catch up with her at any moment, demand that she come with him, and tell her he wanted her no matter what had happened or what she was.

But he hadn't caught up, and by the time she got to the train station cold reason had chilled the heat of her excitement. If Valin had wanted to take her away from her miserable existence, if he intended to heal this terrible breach, he wouldn't have skulked after her and remained concealed.

She plunged from the summit of joy to the depths of wretchedness. Dolly had noticed that Emmie was upset and demanded an explanation. Her friend had been sympathetic and quite willing to lead Valin North on a little chase that would teach him to stay away from Emmie for good.

As she and Dolly got on the train again, she began to wonder what Valin was about. Did he want to catch her in a crime and apprehend her? He'd done that already. No, he was still trying to preserve appearances while getting his damned treasure back. The varmint. He didn't need it; he was just furious that she'd gotten the better of him.

So Emmie had decided to teach Valin a lesson about pride. It hadn't been hard to lead him into the rookeries past a couple of ruffians. She'd been safe the whole time because Snoozer and Sweep had been watching her. She'd gone into one of her hidey-holes and watched the show. Valin had never been in much danger. Any man who could survive the Crimea could handle Toad and Jakes, and her men had been ready to help.

Seeing Valin again in the inadequate glow of gaslights had caused her heart to ache. He was so delightfully handsome, with his clean dark hair, straight soldier's posture, and startling gray eyes. He wore cheap, threadbare clothing as if it were court dress, and—though he was unaware of it— no one would mistake him for an inhabitant of the rookeries. He walked with that air of assurance, taking for granted his power to command, his place in the world. Not even a swell mobsman could emulate that aristocratic bearing, that ease of manner. Certainly all would think twice before disturbing so impressive a man who also wore such a terrifying scowl. Gracious mercy, how she'd missed him.

So, she had watched the encounter with Toad and Jakes, drinking in the sight of him, knowing it would be her last.

She remembered what he'd said: "I don't care if she rots in this cursed place."

Those words still stung. Emmie didn't think she'd ever forget them. How could she when they haunted her dreams?

If he cared, he should have revealed himself. But he was gone, and she felt dead inside. Still, there remained one thing to do. Last night's profits would enable her to send the jewels and coins back to Valin.

Emmie straightened, sighed deeply, and walked to the door. She stuck her head outside and called Pilfer, who was waiting downstairs. Going back to her desk, she picked up an empty wooden shipping box. She had addressed it to Valin at Agincourt Hall. All that remained was to go to the bank and get the treasure so she could put it in the box and mail it.

"Good, Pilfer. You carry this box. We're going to the carriage now."

"Don't wanna go." Pilfer tugged at the collar of

the new shirt she'd bought him. "These shoes hurt."

"Nonsense. They're made of the best leather."

With Pilfer grumbling all the way, Emmie walked to the crossroads where the carriage waited. Pilfer got on the coach box next to Turnip, still complaining. The trip to the bank took a while in the morning traffic. The streets were crowded with supply wagons, omnibuses, and all kinds of coaches and carriages. Once she reached the bank she retrieved the leather case filled with the jewels. As soon as she got to London she'd transferred the gems and coins to a less conspicuous receptacle. Emmie hurried down the white stone steps of the bank, and Turnip helped her into the carriage.

"Hurry," she said. "I want to get rid of this as quickly as possible."

She opened the case. One last glimpse of the only link between her and Valin. Emmie sniffed. She wouldn't cry, not after the wretch had deserted her again. Such reasoning was hardly logical or fair, but Emmie had no desire to be either.

"Uncaring varmint."

The carriage door opened and a glowering Valin sprang into the seat beside her. "Caught you at last! And don't start calling me names."

Emmie's mouth dropped open, but Valin was in the midst of a tirade and wouldn't be stopped.

"You were going to run away again." He tapped the leather case. "Got your hoard and your assistant thieves, and now you're taking them to him."

She scowled at Valin. "What are you doing here?"

"Who is he?"

"Who is who?"

"Don't play the innocent creature with me." Valin loomed over her, frowning like King Arthur confronting Guinevere and Lancelot. "You left me."

Emmie set the jewel case down and tugged at her gloves. "I didn't leave you. I escaped."

"I demand to know who he is, dammit, Emmie!"

Rounding on him, she planted her fists on her hips. "He? He? What are you blathering about?" She stopped, her mouth falling open again in consternation. "Goodness gracious mercy. You think I ran away to be with some man."

"Why else would you run away?"

"Oh, I don't know. Could it be to keep from being thrown in prison?"

"You know I would never do that."

"How would I know that? You made love to me and then ran away as if I'd contaminated you, as if harpies were flying after you, as if the devil were chasing you." Emmie turned and stared straight ahead. "You treated me as if I were a plague carrier."

"And you tricked me, lied to me—twice—and stole from me, *Mrs. Apple*."

Emmie pressed her lips together. He'd discovered her other identity. No use protesting; she was the greater sinner. Why should he wish to connect himself with a lying thief? The silence grew; she had nothing to say that wouldn't reveal how much she longed for him. He didn't want to hear that.

"See here, Emmie. I didn't come to argue. I've seen how you lead your life, and it won't do. You're not going to run about those awful slum courts and stay in that disreputable boardinghouse. You're going to cease purloining other people's paintings and personal adornments. After last night, you must have enough to keep yourself and—and him—in fine style for the rest of your lives."

She hardly listened to what Valin said because it was distressingly clear he wasn't asking her to come with him, that he had no intention of declaring love or even mild affection. Tears threatened to spill onto her cheeks, and she feared she would burst into sobs. He would know then.

Swallowing hard, Emmie picked up the leather case and shoved it at Valin. It hit his stomach hard, and he grunted.

"Here. Take your bloody treasure and get out."

Valin tossed the case onto the opposite seat. "Not until you promise to reform."

Exasperated and desperate to get rid of the man she loved and could never have, Emmie turned a brilliant smile on him and simpered.

"Of course, my lord. I'll stop at once."

"You're not serious."

Emmie turned off her smile and sighed. "I am. Believe me, my lord. I had already planned to leave London and settle in the country. I have a cottage in the North Country with my aunt, Miss Agnes Cowper."

"Give me your word."

"Got a Bible I can swear on?"

"Don't blaspheme. I'll take your word."

"You have it." What was one more lie?

Suffused with pain, Emmie watched Valin get out. She picked up the jewel case as he closed the door. "Don't forget this."

Valin glanced at it without interest. "I didn't forget it. Good-bye, Emmie, my love."

He turned and vanished into the crowd of pedestrians. Emmie sat motionless until Turnip stuck his head in the window.

"You all right, missus? He said he just wanted to talk."

"Yes, Turnip."

"You need a handkerchief?"

"No," Emmie said, fishing in her pocket for her

own. "Drive on, Turnip. We have to mail this parcel and then take Pilfer to the house."

Drawing the curtains, Emmie buried her face in
her handkerchief and wept. Only the necessity of
packing the case in the wooden shipping box enabled her to staunch the flow of tears. Once the
jewels had been mailed she had Pilfer get into
the carriage with her, and they proceeded to the
house.

Upon arriving, both Emmie and Pilfer walked
slowly to the front door. Pilfer's lack of speed
stemmed from his reluctance to leave his life of
adventure; Emmie's came from a great weariness
of spirit and grief. Emmie rang the bell, and the
parlor maid answered with a curtsy and smile.

"Ah-ha!"

Emmie gasped and jumped. "Valin North."

"I knew it." His scowl threatened to conjure up
lightning and black thunderclouds. "I knew you
were lying. Where is he?"

She threw up her hands. "Who?"

"The man for whom you left me."

"You're mad."

"And you're a deceiving lady adventuress. This
is his house, and I demand that you introduce
me."

Emmie had been tapping her foot, her arms
folded across her chest. Suddenly her foot went
still and she gaped at Valin. Understanding flooded

her, and suddenly the entire world seemed beautiful.

"Gracious mercy," she whispered. "You're jealous."

"I think not," Valin snapped.

A grin spread across Emmie's face. "That's why you're glaring at me as if I'd betrayed my country. It's not your foul temper at all. You're jealous!"

Valin nearly shouted. "I am not. I simply disapprove of you connecting yourself with some—some low person. I wish you to mend your conduct and lead a proper, honest life for once."

Emmie just grinned at him, her spirits flying past the highest star. Perhaps there was a chance for her and Valin after all. Valin seemed to grow increasingly uncomfortable under her gaze.

"Are we going to stand here on the step and argue, or are you going to go inside?"

Emmie whirled around and marched past the astonished maid. Pilfer had vanished. Emmie crossed the entry hall and stopped at the foot of the stairs. Valin joined her and stood stiffly, as if awaiting execution.

"You want to see the gentleman for whom I've done all my thieving?"

Valin paled and gave a sharp nod.

"Very well." She looked at the parlor maid. "Is Flash at his studies, Marie?"

"Yes, madam."

"Come with me, my lord."

Emmie nearly danced up the steps.

"Flash," Valin muttered. "Just the kind of name I'd expect of his sort."

She led Valin to a room on the second floor, knocked, and flung the door open.

"Lord Valin, meet Flash. And Phoebe, and Sprout."

Watching Valin's jaw drop gave her enormous satisfaction. He stood there staring at Flash, who stared back. Flash had soft black hair, a heart-shaped face, and great dark brown eyes that seemed to delve into one's soul. He rose from the school table and approached Valin. He extended his hand.

"Please to make your acquaintance, my lord."

Emmie was proud of Flash's manner and cultured speaking voice. She almost laughed aloud at the way Valin gawked at the boy for several seconds before shaking his hand. Phoebe had followed her older brother. She curtsied and slipped her hand into Emmie's.

Valin finally recovered his composure and bowed gravely to the child. "Miss Phoebe, I'm pleased to meet you."

Sprout was still at the school table. He threw his pencil down and jumped up. "Bother! I hate lessons."

Valin looked from Emmie to Sprout and Phoebe and back again.

Emmie held up her hand. "No more absurd speculation." She thanked the children, sent them back to their lessons, and closed the door.

With Valin at her side she went downstairs, into the garden at the back of the house. They strolled between the rose beds.

"Are you ready to hear the truth?" she asked as she clasped her hands behind her back and smiled up at him.

Valin set his mouth in a grim line and nodded.

"They're my stepfather's children."

At this Valin stopped and stared at her. "But you told me your father was a doctor in Shrewsbury. No, don't tell me. That was another lie." Valin sighed. "Where is your stepfather?"

"He's dead."

Emmie embarked upon the story of her mother, Edmund Cheap, and his two families. Valin listened quietly, asking questions only when she paused. At last she had nothing left to say, and Valin remained silent long after her story was finished. After a while Emmie grew uneasy. Had she misunderstood him yet again? Gracious mercy, was he trying to think of a way to extricate himself from her?

Making her tone light, Emmie gazed at a cluster of oak trees while smiling with determination. "So you see why I had to—to pursue my profession. I'm sorry I involved you. I assure you, the gentlemen with whom I usually deal are left with their peace and most of their fortunes intact. Even the Bagshots, the people I visited last night, will hardly notice what I took."

"Emmie."

"And I'm seldom in danger," Emmie hurried on with desperate brightness. "I have many friends and, um, assistants, like Sweep and Turnip and Snoozer. I rub on quite well. It's an exciting life."

"Emmie."

"Flash is going to school in the fall, and Phoebe will have a lady governess. Sprout and Pilfer will study together at first. I'm thinking of buying a bigger house and moving in with the children, and that way—"

"Emmie!"

Valin grabbed her shoulders and forced her to look at him.

Clenching her jaw, Emmie summoned her courage. "Yes?"

"I think you're the bravest, most selfless woman I've ever met."

Her eyes widened. "You do?"

"Indeed. I know you a little, Emmie, my love. It must have cost you dearly to become Mrs. Apple and earn a living in the rookeries. And to take those children under your protection while also supporting yourself was a struggle . . ."

Now she was turning red. "They had no one else. What would have happened to them?"

"I don't want to think about that."

Emmie waited for him to go on, but Valin said nothing. His expression was as bleak as she'd ever seen it, and her new optimism faded. Suddenly Valin turned away from her.

"As long as we're being honest with each other for once, there's something you must know about me."

Emmie touched his arm, and he met her gaze with his anguished one.

"I know," she said. "You can't marry me. I'm illegitimate and a criminal, and I haven't the breeding. I know you can't."

"Don't be absurd. I was talking about me. I did something terrible when I was younger. Something worse than anything you've ever done." Valin gave her a bitter smile. "I have no right to criticize your thieving ways after what I've done. I don't know how I could have been such a hypocrite." He looked down and said softly, "At least you've never killed anyone, and I was responsible for two deaths."

Emmie frowned. "Are you talking about your father and stepmother?"

Valin nodded.

"Oh, Acton tried to make me believe you'd murdered them."

"When?"

"Long ago. Your brother's character is rotten, Valin."

Valin was staring at her. "You didn't believe Acton."

"Of course not. Who believes Acton?"

"But he was telling the truth."

Emmie listened to Valin's story of the note from Carolina, the encounter at the lodge, and the fire. When he finished she shook her head in disgust.

"Have you been blaming yourself all this time?"

"I should have rescued them. I should never have let Father go into the lodge."

Putting the tips of her fingers over Valin's lips, Emmie silenced him. "She made a choice, that Carolina. She made a choice to try to corrupt you. She chose to ignore danger because it gave her a thrill. She chose to do it. You didn't make her do anything, and it was beyond your power to force her to make the proper decisions, or to force your father to see the truth, for that matter."

Emmie stepped away from him and clasped her hands.

"Don't let her evil corrupt your spirit, Valin. Don't blame yourself for their mistakes."

She watched him. He was still frowning.

"You can't save everyone," she said. "It's presumptuous to think you can."

"But I could have—"

"Died trying to save them? Then we never would have met."

Valin seemed locked in a prison of regret. Emmie waited for him to see the reason behind her words, but he said nothing.

Emmie spread her arms wide. "Now you listen to me, Valin North. We've enough sins to regret without taking on more than our share. I certainly have."

Valin gave her a startled look, and at last he laughed. "You certainly do, Mrs. Apple." He came to her and pulled her close. "At least I know your real name now. It will come in handy."

"It will?" She waited for him to explain, but he seemed fascinated with her lips.

"Emmie, may I kiss you?"

Her voice trembled. "I wish you would."

She felt his lips on hers and allowed herself to drown in the embrace. His mouth lifted, and she felt his lips on her cheeks and forehead.

"God, I missed you."

Drawing an unsteady breath, Emmie leaned back to gaze at him. "Now that you know the truth, I wanted to tell you that I understand why you don't want to connect yourself with the likes of me. You need a real lady, someone refined and beautiful who can go about in Society."

"Emmie, shut up."

"Well! I like that. Here I am being reasonable about things, and you—"

He kissed her again, hard. When the kiss ended Emmie scowled at him.

"I don't want you to be reasonable."

Emmie threw his arms off and stalked over to a fountain. "I don't know what you want, varmint."

He came up behind her and surrounded her with his arms. She looked over her shoulder at him. He was grinning at her.

"Emmie, if you would listen a moment, I'll tell you."

"Well?"

"What I want is for you and Flash and Phoebe and Sprout and Pilfer and anyone else in this menagerie of yours to come with me to Agincourt Hall."

"Ha! I've spent years protecting myself against having to depend upon a man for—"

"And I want you to marry me."

"What?" Emmie twisted in his arms and stared at Valin. "What did you say?"

"Will you marry me?"

Catching her lower lip with her teeth, Emmie

whispered. "You can't marry me. You need a wife who—"

"My dear Mrs. Apple. Please allow me to know what I require in a wife, and what I require is Miss Emmie Apple."

"Fox."

"I beg your pardon?"

"Fox," Emmie repeated in a daze. "My name's Emmie Fox, not Apple."

"Are you sure?"

" 'Course I'm sure. Think I don't know me own name? Cheeky bugger."

Valin burst out laughing, which only confused Emmie.

When he stopped and wiped his eyes, he said, "Forgive me, but there's not much to choose between being called Miss Fox and Mrs. Apple."

Emmie grinned at him and took the hand he held out to her. "I suppose you don't like Agnes Cowper either."

"Your aunt? She smirked at me."

"That was me."

"Dear God."

"Want to know my other ones?"

"How many more are there? No, don't answer. Save the revelations for the honeymoon."

"Then let's go find Pilfer."

"He can't come."

"No, I suppose not. But if we don't find him,

he'll scarper back to the rookeries and it will take us weeks to find him again."

Valin's lips hovered above hers.

"Do we have time for a kiss?" he asked.

Emmie wrapped her arms around his neck. "There's always time for a kiss."

About the Author

SUZANNE ROBINSON has a doctoral degree in anthropology with a specialty in ancient Middle Eastern archaeology. She has now turned her attention to the creation of the fascinating fictional characters in her unforgettable historical romances.

Suzanne lives in San Antonio with her husband and her two English springer spaniels. She divides her time between writing historical romance and mystery under her first name, Lynda.

If you loved The Treasure, *don't miss the next delightful romantic adventure from*

SUZANNE ROBINSON

When the clock ticks down on the turn of the century in Edwardian England, it leaves everyone wondering what will be next . . . and whether a sizzling passion will bring in the New Year.

Coming from Bantam Books in spring 2000.

Just in time.